THE
Daybreakers

by the same author

DOWN FROM THE LONELY MOUNTAIN
California Indian Tales

BENEATH THE HILL

THE SLEEPERS

THE CHANGE-CHILD

THE
Daybreakers

JANE LOUISE CURRY

ILLUSTRATED BY
CHARLES ROBINSON

Harcourt, Brace & World, Inc., New York

FOR *Mike* AND *Mark*

THE
Daybreakers

I

Callie slept curled up, like a bear with paws and nose covered or tucked into a good warm spot. If you stretched out straight or turned over, your feet and elbows scritched out onto moon-cold, winter-sharp fields of sheets, as if you were some dream giant sprawled on a snowy hillside. So, once she was nested deep in her cave under the covers, Callie didn't move until dawn. If she dreamed, she never remembered it afterward, though her brother Harry told her she sometimes snorted and snuffled and even talked out loud—things like "You can have my ice cream if you'll shut the window." Harry himself (he was her twin) flopped his arms and legs all over the bed, and groaned, and got his covers all twisted up in knots. When she slept below him in the old bunk beds, it was a little like being on a boat, creaking and swaying, with sails slapping down at you; but here in the new house she had her own room. And sleeping was soft and black and warm as a bear's den—until about six in the morning, anyhow. By then the fire in the furnace, which Mama or Daddy had banked up carefully at bedtime, had died down to a small heart of hot coals in a bed of ashes under the clinker. Awakening inch by inch, Callie felt like the house itself: still warm at the center of her insides, but colder and colder the farther you got from the furnace. Her feet were the front porch and her head the attic, winds rushing under the eaves.

"Brmm. 'Member d' wear socksnasweater d' bed anight," she mumbled into the pillow. Floating gently just under the surface, she heard the muffled words sift down slowly. She dreamed she watched them go by: blurred wisps of words. Her own. She was asleep; and no sooner had that thought swum into her mind than, suddenly, she sat up, fully awake. "And mittens and a scarf!" She yawned and stretched, her eyes wide open. Old Harry would have to take to sleeping in Daddy's mummy bag, the old one he had from the army, if this was what northern winters were like. Callie had never been so cold in her life.

Carefully, so that the bedsprings would not creak, she turned over and pulled her knees up under her. From the head of the bed she could just touch the yarn tassel that hung from the window blind, though it meant getting out into the cold from her warm spot.

It had snowed in the night—and was snowing still, softly and slowly, as if the world were winding down. Like they did on the instant replay of football plays on TV. Winding it down so you could understand the pattern, the intricacy of what was happening, and not have just a fuzzy notion. Slow motion. "Winding down" sounded truer, Callie thought. She pulled Grandma's old patchwork comforter free from the bottom of the bed to wrap around herself. Snow! She had *seen* snow down home in Daingerfield, in Texas, but only falling; never staying like this. Never muffling fields and blanketing the knees of hills, or feathering hillsides and gardens with cut-lace trees, all dim in the white darkness. Because the West Virginia hills shouldered right down to the Ohio River, leaving only a small pocket of a valley for the town of Apple Lock, the snowing world was very small and close and snug. No one would ever guess how browny-gray and ugly it had been such a little time ago. Even the huge slag heap from the S and S Steel mill upriver looked as majestic as the other hills looming over the town. Only balder, of course. Callie sighed. She knew what Harry would say when he saw the snow: "It won't last. Tomorrow it's gonna be as ugly as yesterday. You wanna gush over it, go ahead. *Be* stupid. It's free. Yugh! You won't gush when it's your turn to shovel the driveway." And then he would disappear so as not to have to shovel it himself.

The snow fell as slowly and surely as if the invisible clouds held a winter-long supply, but it fell less thickly than before. Callie could see the hills up back of town, dark against the lightening sky. At the very middle of the top of the Edge, as the crest of the highest hump of the ridge was called, a familiar fringe of naked maple trees was silhouetted against the paling morning, their crowns full of snow. The field at their feet fell away toward Old Edge Road and the Old Dump. Nobody dumped there any more, but it still looked like an avalanche of rusty cans and beer and ketchup bottles suspended over the town—until now. Now all that was blotted out, even the spruce trees Mr. Douglass had planted all along the bottom edge in hopes they might grow tall enough to hide the worst of the mess.

There was a light midway up the hill at the back of the Apple Lock Nursery and Garden Supply. Mr. Douglass's kitchen, Callie thought, though it was too far away and the air too snowy to be sure. Down in the dark town the streetlights were still on, and here and there she could see lights in houses where men who worked the day shift at the mill were up and stirring. What did people *do* when all this snow came dumping down? Below, on Front Street, her answer rumbled out of the garage behind the fire station to wheeze and scrape its way down to Center Street, burying parked cars in heaps of new-plowed snow as it passed. The streetlights winked off. The slow dream-quiet wouldn't last long.

Except, maybe, up above—at the big houses in Ridgeview Heights. And maybe in the deserted wood on the Edge and the dark silver field below it. Nobody ever seemed to go up there, but ever since summer, when the Rivers family had moved to Apple Lock, that high field and its crown of trees had caught Callie's imagination. It wasn't used for anything; no one seemed to know whose it was. It looked kind of lonely and shaggy, Callie thought. Sometimes she called the place the "Dream Wood" to herself because, since nobody paid it any mind, she felt free to make it into whatever she wanted. Trees and field became the hill of Camelot, or the Glass Mountain, or a high plain where elephants and gazelles came crossing and lions walked. She could hear her mother's soft Texas twang in her mind's ear. "Why don't you come away from your daydreaming for once, Callista Lee Rivers? Come on away from that window, hear? Why don't you ever bring some of your little school friends up here? Or if you're so bored with us all, you could go downtown and visit. Wouldn't Mary Lou Washington like to go to that picture show at the Roxy?"

"Oh," Callie could hear herself answer, "who needs Mary Lou Washington? All those kids just sniff and say, 'You think you're something 'cause you live up on the hill, don't you, stuck-up?' You'd think we lived up in Ridgeview or something. Besides, they make fun of the way I talk. *They* just talk about records and TV actors and junk." She never really tried to make Mama understand, any more. "It's not *my* fault. It wasn't my idea we should live up here where there's nobody but honkies."

Boy, did she get it then—with all the Old Familiar Lecture. "You don't want to be called rude things, so you mustn't use disrespectful names to white people." She hadn't used the name *to* anyone, but Mama always ignored that objection. If you got in the habit of using it, she would say, you might say it anywhere and start heaven-knows-what. And embarrass Daddy, who had a difficult enough time, despite the good luck he had, walking straight into a "second helper's" job at S and S the way he did. You could be sure that every white man on the floor was just *waiting* for him to make a mistake, even the ones who'd be sorry if it happened. The big steel companies might have black foremen, even a black man in a desk job here and there, but S and S was smaller, and slow. If they had—or could have found—any other third helper with the experience and seniority to move up, Daddy would never have gotten in. "You know what a risk we took, Callie, Daddy's leaving that job down home because he knew he couldn't get ahead there, and us not knowing I wouldn't find a teaching job up here. So don't you go making things harder than they are, you hear? You don't want to embarrass Daddy, do you?" Of course Callie didn't, and even if it seemed there was something illogical about Mama's argument, it all plopped back in Callie's own lap: Callie, hurt and angry, trying not to cry like a silly baby. All she had meant to do in the first place was distract Mama from harping on her not having a bunch of girl friends to go around with.

Oh, she could always distract Mama: right around in a worrying circle. If only they'd all let her *be*. And today she'd be sure to open her dumb mouth and put her foot in it right on schedule. And Harry had been getting at her all week. She longed to be even, but hadn't been able to think up a really great put-down.

The far-off wood gleamed with the pale light drifting down as softly as the snow. No people up there. What would it be like to have a day in a fresh clean world with nobody else, nobody to muck it all up? Where you wouldn't have to worry what *any*body thought, about how you blew your nose or ate your soup or got excited or whatever.

Swiftly, soundlessly, Callie swung her legs over the side of the bed and scrabbled for her slippers. Once dressed— she put tights on under the blue jeans, and two sweaters over her shirt—she slipped downstairs to the kitchen. Six-thirty, the clock said. Her father would be home in just over an hour unless it was so deep out that he had to wait for a snowplow. When he worked the night turn, like this week, he liked to come home to a hot breakfast and go right to bed; and since Mama slept in on Saturdays, breakfast was Callie's job. She put the kettle on and filled the bottom of the double boiler and put it on to heat, too. Set the table. She hurried. The old toaster down from the cupboard. Brown sugar. Margarine. Soft styrofoam bread. Callie missed Grandma's homemade bread fiercely. This soft, airy gunk wasn't good for anything but mashing into bread pills. It tore when she tried to spread the peanut butter on it, so she settled for making jelly sandwiches. Coffee. Don't forget the salt in the oatmeal. The water foamed out from the bottom of the double boiler, extinguishing the fire and the pilot light. She relit it and then took a spoon to the oatmeal, trying to squash the lumps out. No one was stirring overhead, and so Callie had a cup of coffee with her toast and cereal. It was almost half milk, the way Grandma used to fix it for her when Mama wasn't looking.

After going down to the cellar to poke up the fire and put some more coal on, Callie brought her coat and warm hood from the hall to put them on in the kitchen. Everything was ready for her father to heat up when he came. It wouldn't be as good as fresh, but he wouldn't mind just this once. So far so good. She wrapped the sandwiches and put them in her coat pocket. On the cold back porch she pulled on her boots and mittens and then went wading out to the garage, where she remembered seeing an old broad shovel laid up across the rafters. There were about six inches on the ground already, but the driveway was short and steepish, so it wasn't hard to clear. Under Harry's window she scraped the shovel loudly across the cement just to make sure he stayed in bed and didn't come bothering her. The town snowplow went past when she was almost to the bottom, dumping a knee-high wall of snow all along the curb. That slowed her down, but she had finished and was hurrying along South Hill toward Old Edge Road before there was any sign of her father.

A day off from people.

"Ee-eyou!" She took a running start and slid sideways on the tightly packed snow where the plow had passed.

As Callie went by the Nursery and Garden Supply, she could see Mr. Douglass already at work potting geraniums from the flats she had helped him set out for rooting before school started. She clambered over the drift where the plow had turned to head downhill again. Maybe, with Christmas not far away and with school being on half session because of the school district going broke, she could get a job afternoons making Christmas wreaths or something. There was a three-slices-at-once toaster her mother would like, but so far Callie had saved up only three dollars. Turning up Old Edge Road, she was doing addition with each step, ringing up enough for a little electric drill, too, for the workshop her father talked about setting up in the cellar.

"That's a lot of wreaths, silly." She laughed at herself with a gasping wheeze and turned to face downhill, hands on knees, to catch her breath. The snowy air had wrapped close around her, and, preoccupied, Callie had not noticed how far she had come, how fast. No plow and no traffic would be coming up this way. The road was narrow and dangerously full of chuckholes, but it was easy to follow even under all the snow because nothing else was so level. Not far beyond the second bend above the nursery, she slowed, wondering whether she had come too far. The road no longer climbed. She knew she must be somewhere below the cemetery. Turning, she hopped back, trying to keep in her own footprints. Already they were filling up.

Wind drifted the snow downhill, baring tussocks of grass on the slope above. Leaving the road, Callie began to climb. It was hard going—like running in deep sand. Once she fell and slid down a steep place she had just spent five minutes climbing up.

"You telling me to clear off, hill?" She laughed into the wind. "Not me, old hill. You look out, you hear?"

At the top of the steep place she saw that she had come into the field below the Dream Wood and that it was broader and not so steep as it looked from South Hill. There was no wind now, only the snow falling, erasing all the movement and sound in the town below. The tracks she made as she headed for the trees seemed strange and out-of-place, a straggling line of obscure hieroglyphs on a white page.

The trees stood tall, a wall along the field's crown, dark trunks fading through gray to ghostly tree-shapes in the wood's depth. The air and the wood were so full of snow that Callie decided to leave exploring for another day. It would be too easy to get turned around in there. Besides, its white gloom made her shiver unaccountably. It wasn't a shiver from the snow down her boots or the wet blue jeans, though they were icy-cold against her backside. It was a shudder that shook her as if someone had placed a cold hand between her shoulders, under her shirt. She turned her back on the wood and looked out over the white world.

"Yo, here I am!" she shouted, but the sound was deadened, muffled in the snowfall. "Hey, you town! You look real pretty stretched out in your new shroud, don't you? But I know it isn't so, you hear? You're a dirty, smelly, cold old place, and I hate you, hear? You hear?" she yelled. "You can't touch me up here!"

The snow fell away, dying into the Dream Wood, darker now, clearer and very still, as if it waited some sound or sign.

"You're nothing either," Callie called to the trees. "You're nothing unless I *let* you be. You give me any lip, trees, and I'll dream you into firewood. I'll conjure you clean away, you hear?"

Anger, welling out of nowhere, blurred the trees before her eyes, and a store of discontents long brushed out of sight into the corners of her mind stirred as if in answer to something in the wood.

Callie kicked at the snow, and a ball of it rolled, gathering size and speed across the sloping field, disappearing over the rise downhill toward the road.

"Hoy!"

She kicked again and then, looking around, made sure there was no one watching. There hardly would be. Yet she felt the prickle of watching eyes, a prickle at the nape of her neck. There was only the cemetery to the south, and on the other side of the wood must be Ridgeview Park and the golf course. The nearest houses in Ridgeview Heights must be a quarter mile or more from where she stood. She shrugged the thought away.

Beginning at the south end of the field, she rolled a small ball across, bringing it at last, a snow boulder too large to move farther, to a spot near the trees at the upper end. A second, smaller one she brought to place on top of it. The fresh snow was so light and feathery that the balls were very delicate, easily shattered, and had to be supported underneath in the rolling and lifting. It was hard to get the knack of it. With handfuls of snow to fasten the two spheres together and shape the arms, she managed at last, and after an hour the snowman was as tall as herself and lacked only a head. Callie left him without one while she made a second figure, and then a third. It was time-consuming work, but the building went more quickly after she gave up on the large balls and used smaller ones about a foot in diameter, molding them together with loose snow. Seven. She must make seven.

A wind came up while she worked. It stripped the last of the faded red leaves from the top branches of the wood, scattering them down the field and then drifting the powdery snow over them. The snow blew down Callie's neck and chilled her wrists as it crusted over her mittens. Her watch read nearly noon, and she was tired. Snowflakes caught in her eyelashes, and the wind snatched her breath away.

"It's like smothering," she thought, panicky. "If I can't breathe deep, just once, I'll smother!" The strange thought crossed her mind that she must not smother before the seven snowmen had heads. "Weird-o!" she wheezed, but she was really a little bit alarmed.

After a while the wind veered around to the north, so that the wood afforded her some protcetion. She fashioned seven snowballs as heads for the lumpy figures; and from a lone fir tree and one of the smaller maples at the wood's edge brought boughs from which to break bits for crowns and wands. Thicker twigs, broken short and pushed into the snow, made beady eyes and beaky noses. With a T-shaped twig, the stem pushed straight in, Callie found that she could make a pretty good mouth. Depending on the way the crosspieces bent, the blank, staring faces suddenly frowned, set stubbornly, or smirked. The figures stood in a semicircle around her: stolid, formal, somehow threatening. The wind died away, but the snow fell steadily.

"Hah! You better not look at me like that, hear? I can kick you down faster'n I put you up."

Wrapping her coat tightly around her, Callie sat down in a well-trampled spot and pulled the sandwiches from her pocket. Both were squashed flat, and it was like eating jelly dough, but she was so hungry that it didn't matter. She was tired, and they were delicious.

The seven white shadows in the white darkness watched impassively, as if they waited and listened. Callie had forgotten them, her world shrinking to the sweet and gummy delight of eating very fast, with no one to caution about chewing thoroughly and not gulping. The snowmen, masked for a moment by a gust of snow, seemed when next she looked to have forgotten her in turn. She began to wish she had not made them. Their sharp twig eyes stared eerily over her head toward the trees, and Callie imagined that they leaned, hunched in a dreadful urgency, to catch some word in the wood.

"I think I'm gonna knock you all down in a minute," she announced thoughtfully through a mouthful of sandwich. "You were a dumb idea anyhow." But as she finished the last bit and pulled her mittens on again, she heard a sound that froze her, too, into a listening silence.

It was a series of high-pitched squeaks, strung together in a thin scream. Desperate, and yet distant, it rang on the highest edge of hearing, strange and despairing.

Callie ran, plunging through the drifts toward the wood's edge. The sound wavered and then stopped, but she was sure it had come from the midpoint, where the ground

under the wood's eaves rose highest. Bursting up through a snowy briar tangle, she found herself on the edge of a flat, squarish rise where no trees stood.

In its center sat a small, thin boy: hatless, barehanded, pale, with hair more white than blond, and strange, washed-out blue eyes. He looked at her unseeing. From one thin hand a small rabbit swung limply.

It had been the rabbit screaming.

2

Turning and rising in one whirling, darting movement, the child whipped through the tangled blackberry briars and into the snowy wood.

"Here, you! You, kid! You drop that rabbit, hear?" Callie shrieked into the thick silence. "Hey!"

He couldn't have come from far away—not dressed like that. She plunged after him. Despite the snow and cold, he had no coat, only a sweater, and wore—she was sure she had not imagined it—only thin slippers on his feet. Callie stumbled, caught herself, and crashed on through the underbrush along the crest of the tree-clad hillock.

"You drop that poor thing, you mean little sneak!" she shouted, gasping between each word. Clambering over a fallen tree trunk, Callie could see where the boy had slithered under it. A few yards farther she took a bad tumble where drifting snow disguised a sudden dropping away beneath her feet of the higher ground. The boy must have made an unbelievable leap or swung down on a tree branch, for his footsteps left off and took up again beyond.

"What you want to hurt it for?" she yelled. "Leave it be!"

The boy was almost gone from sight, vanishing in the maze of dark tree trunks and snow-masked bushes and reappearing farther on, a wispy shadow in the white air. Callie was crying, for she had begun to be as frightened by what she had seen as angered. She followed the tracks to a split-rail fence and climbed over it. Snow had fallen down the tops of her boots and melted. Her feet were cold and heavy, too clumsy for her to catch up with him. It was like waking from a dream, rising slowly to the real world while the dream sped on into the dark. How could he go so fast? She wiped her nose, dripping with the cold, on the back of a mitten. The kid would be all the way to Ridgeview Heights by now. The snow fell heavily, blurring Callie's own trail behind her. She was unsure how far she had come.

"Stinking little weasel. You let loose that rabbit! What'd it ever do to you?" The words came as raggedly as her breath, and she could not see for the snowflakes on her lashes. "Miserable . . . toadstool." Callie leaned against a tree and tried to catch her breath. "C-cockroach! Lousy . . ."

"Larva? And maggot . . . mean, maggoty stinkwort."

The voice came out of nowhere. Callie peered around, astonished.

"Maggoty *stinkwort?*"

"I think it's something like skunk cabbage. And he *is* maggoty. I think his mother found him under a rock."

Callie looked up. A familiar face hung out from the branches directly overhead: red-nosed and splotched with the cold; damp wisps of blond hair straggling out from a tartan hood. Callie squinted upward in bewilderment. For a moment it seemed as if she were slipping back into a dream, but then the apparition drew out a crumpled handkerchief and blew its nose.

"Melissa Mitchell!" said Callie faintly. "What the heck you think you're doing up a tree in a snowstorm?"

"It's a tree house, dumbbell. I bring crumbs and junk out

here for the birds. What were you yelling at the Drip for?"

"Don't you 'dumbbell' *me*. You're the one flunked the old math test yesterday, not me." Callie sniffled and tried to keep her voice from shaking. "Drip? Come on, who's this Drip?" She watched Melissa maneuver for a backward descent from the rickety tree house. "I thought you were too stuck up to call a good name. 'His mama found him under a rock.' Hoo! I got to remember that one next time Harry calls me . . . well, next time he calls me anything. Who *is* this Drip of yours?"

"He's not mine. Or not *truly*." Melissa wrinkled her nose. "He's my cousin, and his name's Conway, but everybody calls him Sonny. Isn't that awful? Sonny Tapp. Drippy Tapp."

Callie looked pained.

"Well, it fits. You know, he looks about four, but really he's seven. I thought he was home sick in bed. He's supposed to be. What was he doing?"

Callie eyed her doubtfully. Mama always said, "Now, don't you go upsetting people. Just you keep your mind to yourself." But if she did that, she'd explode. Besides, even if he was Melissa's cousin, she had called him a larva herself.

"He was tormenting this little rabbit. It was screaming. I think maybe he killed it."

"Well, come on then! He'll drop it somewhere. He'd never let Grandpa catch him with it. Or if he does, he'll tell Grandpa *I* did it, and I'll catch what for." Melissa hurried off through the trees.

Callie followed, more slowly. "Why should *I* come," she called. "That's *your* problem, Me-lissa Mit-chell."

Melissa stopped. "But . . . I thought you wanted to help the bunny rabbit."

"*Bunny* rabbit?" Callie mocked.

"OK, 'rabbit.' Now who's stuck up?" Melissa looked resentful. "What were you chasing Sonny for, then?"

Callie shrugged. "I dunno. I guess the rabbit's dead. I s'pose I just wanted to beat on him like he did on it."

"Well, come *on!* Maybe we can catch him still." Melissa pulled her along by her sleeve.

Callie followed, but that cracked her up. In a few yards she was laughing so hard that her breath caught in hiccups and she had to stop. Melissa looked mad, as if to say, "Make up your darned mind," but soon she had caught it, and the two of them were giggling like idiots, swinging themselves around the young trees.

"Two big old girls . . ."

"Mean as mean . . ."

"With clubs to whack with!"

"Catching a little shrimp . . ."

"Of a shrimp! . . ."

They fell into a chant.

"On the front doorstep . . ."

"Whomping him . . ."

"Into peanut butter."

"Who, *me?* Why, I never . . ."

"Laid a finger on him. We *wouldn't* . . ."

"*Do* such a thing."

They threw their arms around the trees and hung there, laughing.

"Hey, I'll call you 'Callie,' like your brother does, and you call me 'Liss.' I hate 'Melissa.' *It's* stuck up: a bunch of pink ribbons and curls all stuck together with corn syrup. Like Angela Paff."

"Yugh! Her! OK. But whoever heard of 'Liss' for a name?"

"That's why I like it."

They walked on slowly.

Liss grinned. "You know what old Angela Paff called you? You and Mary Lou Washington and Erna La Farge? *Darkies!* Like you were something out of old Stephen Corn-Syrup Foster."

"That's all right," said Callie with a superb air of condescension. "Angela Paff may be only eleven, but already she's one of the Old Folks at Home."

Liss hooted.

And then they found the rabbit.

"No, Mama, I don't mean he was white; I mean he was *white*. Like, if he only had pink eyes, he'd've been an albino, I suppose. Pass the corn bread, please, Daddy?"

Callie's mother pushed her chair back and leaned down to retrieve the napkin she had dropped. "Oh, Callie, you *didn't* chase after him!"

Callie slathered the corn bread with butter. "Don't worry. We didn't catch him. After we buried the rabbit in a hole we found in their back garden, Liss sneaked in and found him in bed, in his pajamas, moaning away like a sick puppy, with his nurse fussing all over him. Liss says he hid the wet clothes on top of a hot-water heater in a hall closet, so's they'd dry fast."

"Hey, that's bad, man," Harry said admiringly. "You mean this little kid's got white hair? The whole bit?"

"Mm-hmm." Callie shivered. "He gave me the creeps."

"Aah, you creep pretty easy." He scoffed, spreading his ham loaf with mashed potatoes and digging into it with relish.

"Harry! Don't *do* that. Don't you have any manners at all? Leon, will you tell your son his potatoes aren't for slathering all over his meat?"

Mr. Rivers retrieved the platter of corn bread and took another piece. "My son, your potatoes aren't for slathering all over your meat," he said.

28

Callie and Harry exchanged grins.

"You hear?" their father said.

"Oh, man!" Harry grumbled but scraped the potatoes to one side.

Mr. Rivers had been listening with interest to Callie's story and now returned to it. "Was it because he was sick that he wandered out like that? Sometimes people do look and act strange when they're ill."

"Maybe. I don't know. He was such a funny kind of white: sort of . . . transparent. Not at all like a picture I once saw of a real albino. But that one was an African, and he looked . . . well, *flat* white, almost like he'd been sprayed. This Sonny looked like he'd been, well, *drained* white. You know what I mean? And I don't think he's just sick. I think he's sick in the head."

"Callie!"

"Heck, Mama, Liss said so, too."

"Well, you shouldn't repeat it, you hear?"

"She won't," her father said.

Callie eyed him uncertainly and then looked fixedly at her plate. The words came out in a torrent. "Daddy? I hated him. I got so mad I might of really busted him one if I caught him. It was . . . it was like him killing that rabbit was all the meanness in the world at once, and I couldn't help it. I wanted to hurt him so *bad*." While she spoke, she carefully mixed her potatoes and gravy into a brownish mess.

"So badly," Mrs. Rivers amended automatically, twisting her napkin in agitation. She looked at her husband.

Mr. Rivers looked at Callie and took another bite of corn bread while he thought what to say. "Do you want me to tell you it's wrong to be angry?" he asked at last. "No-o. I suppose you might even say it can be a very good thing. *If* it makes you try to straighten things out; to change what makes you mad." He buttered the last bite of bread thoughtfully, eyeing her innocently. "I suppose this little boy, once you had thoroughly clobbered him, would have seen the light? Sworn off tormenting small animals and cousins? Dedicated his life to helping decrepit old ladies across streets?"

Harry laughed at his sister's discomfiture. Callie, who had half expected a stern lecture and was prepared to feel nobly penitent, giggled into her napkin.

"No," she admitted. "I s'pose I would've felt better. But only for a little while, I guess." She slouched down in her chair and fetched a sigh. "Why has everything always got to be so complicated?"

Mr. Rivers turned to his wife. "You know who those children's Grandpa is, don't you, Marie? It's the big stone house up there with towers like a castle, isn't it, Cal? That's old Senator Tapp. Somebody up at the plant was saying he's the meanest old cuss in ten counties, and him close onto eighty at that." He hesitated. "I don't think you ought to fool around up there, hon. How come you know this Liss anyhow?"

"Oh, she's in my sixth grade." I guess she's the only one from the Heights who still comes down to Fourth Street since we had to go on half-day. All the rest go to Holy Name or that church school up on the Heights."

"Didn't they cut that school bus out even before the district lost the school bond vote?" asked Mrs. Rivers.

"Yes'm, I guess so. Do you suppose that's why people didn't vote any money for school? Because so many kids don't go to the public schools any more, and still their parents were having to pay for them and the other schools, too?"

Mr. Rivers speared a piece of ham loaf. "That's what they say."

Harry caught the ironic tone that Callie missed, and scowled.

Callie shrugged. "I guess Liss must catch a ride with someone. Can I have some more green beans?" She helped herself.

" '*May* I,' " said her mother absentmindedly.

"Cal," her father said slowly, "I think you'd better stay clear of the Tapp house. It sounds a pretty unhappy place to me. And I don't want them to . . . make you unhappy."

Callie helped her mother clear the dishes and brought in plates and forks for the cake. "I don't guess I'll worry," she said. "It was kind of a weird day, but I liked it. I was really *awake,* and most of this old town is dead as dead."

"You can say that again." Harry took his cake into the living room and turned up the TV. The Oilers were playing the Buffalo Bills at Houston, and a half hour of silent play viewed from his dining room chair was all he could stand. "Man, I wish I was down there now. Look at old 76 take that big one out. Righteous, man!"

Callie sighed. Good old Saturday night. After the game and the dishes there was "Get Smart," but nothing much else: a kind of clunky ending for such a strange day. A weird day. She turned her mind away from a whisper deep inside—an echo of a poem she had read?—that said tomorrows only come because todays change so many things.

"No! Catch me going back up there? They've got nothing to do with me. Heck, I don't care a bean about her skinny, runty cousin," Callie announced silently and firmly to the dish towel.

She was still reading under the covers with a flashlight at midnight when a strange, slithering, shlumphing sound finally broke through her concentration. She switched the flashlight off and stuck her head out. The house was quiet.
Shlumph.
The silence that followed was almost worse than the

*shlumph*ing. Callie's mind raced. There wasn't any *drip-drip*, so it couldn't be a thaw, so it couldn't be snow sliding off the roof. She wriggled toward the bedpost by the window. Looking up through the gap between blind and sill, she could see a corner of the eaves, hung with icicles, sharp and fat. And not a drip.

Shlumph-ph.

She couldn't raise the blind. If someone was monkeying around the garage, he would see the movement. If there was someone, she could yell for her father, but a caution rooted in the strangeness of the sound made her slide from the bed and slip to the other window, where the blind was halfway up. She mustn't be seen. She knelt by the window, shivering.

Shlumph-umph.

In the darkness the forgotten nightmare wildness of the snowy noon swept back, filling the room behind her with shapes and the world outside with heavy shufflings heard only dimly through the glass.

"You sure creep easy!" She whispered, mocking at herself, remembering Harry's taunt. The bubble of a laugh that raised in her throat made it easier to raise her head above the sill and look out onto the back yard and the steep slope of South Hill.

It was still snowing: big, fat flakes scudding slantways with the wind. Only a corner of the garage was visible, but it was lit by the streetlight and apparently deserted. The kitchen garden immediately below the window was white and empty.

"*Callie?*" She heard her name. Someone calling. But it was only in her head, a call with no sound or shape.

And then something moved—or seemed to—up under the two large fir trees that spread their drooping, overlapping arms across the upper end of the yard. The boughs trailed on the ground with the weight of the snow, making the trees more like a huge two-masted tent than ever; and behind the screen of snow and black boughs, shadows moved.

Callie counted seven: wavering shadows, bulky, indistinct in shape, and crowned. Searching with blind eyes. She shrank back to the floor, sure that they could see even a black face at a dark window. And she knew who they were searching for.

There were seven snowmen in the yard.

3

"Where are you going, honey?" Callie's father lowered the Sunday *Press* as he saw her sidle past the living-room door with her coat on.

Callie had survived church and Sunday lunch, torn between the urge to tell someone about the dream and an uneasiness, a mistrust, that made her hold her tongue. At least she *hoped* the snowmen had been a dream. Before church, while her father had been warming up the car, she had gone up into the back yard to look at the ground under the fir trees. The snow was churned up, and there seemed to be some sort of track leading down from the straggly woods above. But then there were a lot of dog tracks, too, and what she guessed were cat or rabbit tracks, maybe both. So you couldn't really tell.

"Oh, up on the Edge, I guess. No, not to see that girl," she said evasively, seeing his slight frown. "Why should I? She's nothing special. It's just . . . I want to look for something up there—something I had up there yesterday. I think I might've lost it." It was true, in a sneaky sort of way.

"Mm. Well, don't be too late." He turned back to the paper.

Callie hurried back to the hall, buttoning her coat, her thoughts in a jumble. *Could* the snowmen have moved? Gotten lost? Maybe they weren't hers to lose. If they had been here and gone, why then they had found themselves, Callie thought, a little wildly. They were their own. Last night they had bowed and smiled their thin-lipped smiles and beckoned . . .

Harry was in the kitchen with the TV sports section spread out on the table. The Jets were playing the San Diego Chargers and the Giants were up against the Rams, but neither game would get going until four o'clock, and both Eddie Williams and Mel Brown were in bed recovering from the flu. Harry looked up, bored.

"Where you going?"

Callie called from the porch as she slammed the back door. "Nowhere."

Harry stuck his head out. "I bet *I* know, Aunt 'Tash'!" he sang after her.

"Oh, shut up and let rigor mortis set in," she yelled.

With a little jump she skated down the driveway, but a rough spot near the bottom tripped her up and she landed in a heap. Harry's laughter followed her up the street. She stalked on without looking back and so missed seeing him come out a few minutes later, coat collar up and the warm flaps of his cap down, to follow her.

It was a good afternoon for walking. The sun shone brightly, and there were very few clouds. The trees along the roadside glistened, and snow fell from the branches with soft *phlumphs*, pocking the snow on the ground with little holes. The deserted field below the Edge glittered in the sunlight, so that Callie had to shade her eyes and even then could not see clearly. Snow and trees wavered in the shimmer and glare. But the surface where she walked was churned and rough, and as she moved uphill, she found that the entire field was crisscrossed with broad, wavering lines that caught the sunshine. They were crunchy underfoot despite the warm glare, and they looked like great, slithery snail tracks. Callie shivered and half turned as if to go no farther, but then—almost against her will, drawn by curiosity or some obscure demand—turned back and ran toward the field's far end.

The snowmen were gone. Where they had stood, green grass flamed in seven ragged patches.

Callie stood staring, dumbfounded: no melted heaps, only bare grass. For yards around, the snow was trampled, but nowhere were there heaps or any sign that boys or dogs or . . . anything . . . had rolled them away or knocked them down. Helplessly, unsure whether to laugh or run, she wheeled to scan the field and the gray wood.

At the wood's far edge near the cemetery's stone wall a red scarf flickered.

"Callie! It's me, Liss!"

The small figure beckoned.

"Oh, spit!" Callie muttered. How could she *tell* anyone about the snowmen? Telling a thing, putting it into words, somehow made it more real and harder to turn your back on. But how could she *not* tell anyone? It was so weird. And all things considered, Liss might be better to tell than Harry. Harry would hoot her to Wheeling and back.

She waved.

"Oh, hurry up!" Liss called, flapping her arms in a fit of impatience. "Come see."

Callie slowed. What if it were the snowmen? The thought that they might now be standing stolidly within the wood, seven innocent snow figures, easy to smash and

36

trample, made her feet drag. If they had moved and were still only snow and twigs . . . why, it would be worse than ever, because there could be no explanation. Her curiosity shriveled.

But it was not that. Liss had found something else. She had come out intending to follow yesterday's tracks to find just where Sonny had gone and perhaps why. But most of the trail had disappeared, and not from the snow's drifting or the present thaw. The snowy floor of the wood was much as it had been the day before, for the maples, young and old together, grew so thickly that the sun fell only scantily there and the air was chill.

"So how could all *this* be *melted?*"

Liss waved her hand dramatically toward the narrow hillock that stretched itself behind the wood's eaves along the crest of the Edge. For the moment Callie forgot her snowmen.

The long mound was bare of snow. Tree-clad, lapped over by the wood, it rose out of the snow: wet, leaf-carpeted, matted in places with briars and fallen branches.

"Oh!"

It was as if the shared excitement freed her from the morning's shadows. She moved more freely and flapped her arms in bewilderment.

"I don't *know*. It was thick as thick yesterday."

Liss gestured excitedly. "It looks like somebody melted a big, fat streak with one *whoosh* of a monster hair dryer."

"Noo-o. . . . It's more like your old hump had—what do they call it?—'radiant heating'?"

"It's not *my* old hump," Liss contradicted. "It gives me goose bumps. I mean, I don't understand." Her eyes widened. "Do you suppose it's a *sign?*"

"Of what?" Callie scoffed. Yet she knew what Liss meant. There was a strange attraction to the place, something that would not let you turn your mind away. She climbed the bank and walked along the mound's crest, through the trees and brush.

"Well, there's got to be a reason for it, hasn't there?" Liss hopped along behind. "And reasons are for figuring out."

"I s'pose." Callie answered absentmindedly. "Here's where I found your cousin yesterday." She pointed.

Liss scuffled at the soggy leaves with her boot. "It's wider here. Brr, and colder, too." She clapped her arms.

Callie shrugged, frowning. The spot had an ugly feel to it, heavy, demanding. The cold lodestone pulling at metal, drawing it to rest imprisoned near the stone's heart. Her mouth had a bitter, metallic taste to it, an angry taste, and she had to bite back words that slid onto her tongue—sharp knives of words that said any splotchy idiot could feel that cold was cold and see that width was wide, so what else was new? Callie's lips moved in an awkward way, trying to keep to words that would not wound. "Maybe. But you get cold when you slow down. Come on away." She hurried along the mound, pulling free of the hateful cold. "Look, it's melted the same way all along here. What's a long, skinny sausage of a hill doing up here anyhow?"

Liss looked back the way they had come. "It does look kind of like an overgrown gopher tunnel, doesn't it? But it must be old as old. The trees are as big here as they are in the rest of the wood . . ." She broke off. "Callie! What—what is it?"

Callie had turned to speak as she approached the end of the mound when, abruptly, the ground underneath gave way and she found herself almost up to the waist in damp, crumbly earth and wet leaves. The jarring drop drove the breath from her lungs, and the only sound she could manage was a panicky one somewhere between a squeak and a snort.

38

"Here, give me your hand." Liss dug her heels in and pulled while Callie strained up on tiptoe in her hole.

"It's no good. I can't get a foothold." She wailed. "It feels like I'm standing on a wobbly stone, and the rest is just air. Uhnh. It teeters. Wait a minute. Let go for a minute."

Liss stood back and was puzzled to see Callie bend forward from the waist to lie as flat against the ground as possible. The face she made showed the effort it took to draw her knees up a few inches in the restricted hole and swing her heels backward to catch a foothold behind her.

"OK," she gasped, reaching out. "Grab ahold. I can push now."

When at last she was out of the hole, she was breathless and covered with damp earth and leaves. Liss brushed at her coat.

"Don't jiggle up and down so. I'll get your coat all smeary if you don't hold still, silly. There. You'd better wait until the rest is dry before you brush it off, or it'll never come out."

"I know." Callie was excited and impatient. "Never mind about that. You know what's down there? It's *got* to be a *cave*. I was flapping my dumb old legs around, and they didn't hit *any*thing until I oompsed up higher. What if it *is* a cave? Or the entrance to a great huge one? And *I* found it!" She got down on her knees and peered into the hole but could see nothing, so then she stretched out flat to hang her head over the edge.

"Hey! I just brushed you all off."

Callie stuck an arm down. She could feel nothing but the earthen walls up near the opening. "Nothin' but hole," she panted.

Liss sat on her heels beside her, taking care not to kneel on the wet leaves. "You know, there are a couple of little phosphorescent caves in the hill along Apple Ridge Road.

We used to shine flashlights in so we could see the rocks glow afterwards. Mother made me promise I'd never go in one. They're dangerous. You're just lucky this one caved in under you instead of *on* you."

"Flashlights. That's what we need." Callie scrambled up. "You got one at home?"

"Of course we do." Liss leaned gingerly over the hole. "But you probably wouldn't see anything but your teetery stone down at the bottom."

"Um. I suppose." Callie measured with her eye the distance from the hole to the point where the mound sloped down to the level of the surrounding wood. It looked to be no more than eight or ten feet.

"We could dig us a bigger hole, coming out this way toward the low ground. That'd give us a look-in, wouldn't it?" Her eyes were wide with an excitement deeper than she could account for. "The air down in that hole was *warm*. Talk about *signs*! First there was that poor cottontail, and then the snowmen luring me up here again. Now here's this mound-thing . . . well, *showing* itself. You felt how creepy-cold it was back there a ways; and now this." She took a deep breath. "My head's going 'round in circles with it all. None of it makes sense but, like you say, it's *got* to: 'Reasons are for figuring out,' you said." Her mouth set in a stubborn line.

"Snowmen?" Liss looked at her doubtfully. "Are you sure falling down that hole didn't jiggle your brains loose? What snowmen?"

Callie explained, but of course it did seem senseless. Here at the caved-in hole there was no cold or heaviness, none of the compelling anger of the other spot. And, blessedly, no white shadows in the wood, either. Callie began to suspect a lot of it had been her own imagination. Liss, of course, cheerfully brushed aside the silly idea that there could be any connection between the missing snowmen and the mound. She was eager to talk about caves.

Callie said, "We saw a couple of really big ones in Missouri when we came north last summer: rooms as big as our whole school, and stone icicles, and all." She looked sideways at Liss. "A couple of kids discovered one of them. By accident."

"And you think . . ." Then Liss laughed, catching Callie's look. "Oh, cut it out. Look, I'll run home for the flashlight, and we can use the shovel out of the garden house. You come if you want to, but I can't ask you in. Not today, anyhow."

Callie straightened. The hostility of the slight movement flustered Melissa, and she hastened to explain.

"No, it's the Drip. Sonny. He had a fever all last night and kept yelling somebody was calling him to come out. Nutty stuff. Anyhow, everybody's been tiptoeing around all day, and Grandpa's in a foul temper."

"I'll wait here. No sense both of us going." Callie turned her attention back to the hole, hiding her alarm. She almost asked if the screwy little boy had dreamed of snowmen, too, but held her tongue. He was no business of hers.

Liss hesitated, biting her lip. But then she turned and ran to the mound's end and down into the snowy wood.

Harry had come along the cemetery wall and was hanging out of sight behind a screen of trees when she returned twenty minutes later. He had watched Callie clearing the leaves away and now saw the girls take turns at digging the hole wider, but he was too far away to hear anything. He could not puzzle out what they were up to. His sister crawled halfway into the hole they had been digging at, and what's-her-face, the white girl, handed down a large battery lantern. There was some kind of confusion—an argument, he guessed—and Callie's legs kicked and wriggled out of sight. After a moment's hesitation the other girl got down and followed.

They didn't come out right away, so Harry slipped closer, passing along the deep woods' side of the mound. Some nut, he observed, had built seven snowmen around a tree at the midpoint of the long hillock. But it was even odder that while these stood in a little drift of snow, all the rest of the high ground had melted. At least, that explained why the girls had been able to dig so quickly. He felt himself drawn toward the hole as if it were a magnet and he an iron filing. It was bigger than he had thought. The girls had only dug a little after all; the rest had fallen in. They had gone in head first, wriggling down the sloping heap of dirt and rocks: there was no other way it could be managed. Harry watched the hole, fighting his rising curiosity.

Ten minutes, and then fifteen, and they did not come out. He began to worry. He called. There was no answer. That did it. Sticking his hat in his coat pocket, he knelt, then lay flat and squirmed his way in.

Once past the dirt and rockfall, he found the passage smooth and dry, walled and roofed with stone. It was about three feet high and angled slightly downward. Raising up, he felt his way along on hands and knees, carefully.

"Cal? Hey, Callie! You all right? It's me."

The words reverberated in his ears. It was as if he were suspended in a dark echo chamber.

"Where *are* you?"

His hand touched metal, and he flinched. It was only the big flashlight. But why had they left it here? Harry fumbled for the button and switched it on.

He found himself in a small rock-walled chamber. It was a dead end. There was no way out but the way in. And the girls were not there.

4

The passage, once the girls were past the rubble and the dirt pile, was warm and dry. Callie did not think to switch the flashlight on. Raising herself to her hands and knees, she felt ahead and then moved on. Liss was close behind. Apparently the cave-in had been occasioned by the collapse of a portion of the roof. The stone-arched passage gave way to a larger space. The walls drew away, and Callie's outstretched hand fell against the air. Liss squeezed through beside her.

"What is it? Why'd you stop? Hey, I found something! Something hard and flat."

Callie fumbled with the light. "Just a minute."

A low, domed room flared up out of the darkness. In the center of the floor was spread a long, low heap of stones or objects blurred with a heavy, ages-long covering of fine dust. Liss twisted onto her side to hold her hand in the lamp's light, and Callie whistled between her teeth. Liss's find was a flat, round disk of bronze, inlaid with a design in some metal now black with tarnish. Scraped with a finger-nail, it looked to be silver. The pattern was simple, almost crude, but delicately executed, and the border was richly engraved.

"Treasure!"

The girls looked at each other in astonishment for a moment and then scrambled on their knees toward the dusty heap. Callie set the flashlight down and reached for an object at the edge of the pile.

"Look at this. A cup, made out of a big seashell!"

"And here's a funny bowl. It's stone, with carved squirrels running around the edge! Who do you suppose all this stuff could belong to?"

Callie stretched her hand out toward a rich blue-green stone that gleamed in the light. As Liss pulled impatiently at Callie's sleeve, her elbow knocked the lamp over. It blinked out at the same moment that Callie's hand closed around the stone.

Both saw the light die out as a strange gathering-to-itself, the enveloping circle falling away, shrinking to a coin, a pearl, a pinprick, and winking out, and with it the cave, the treasure, the world. A wind rushed in their ears, and they fell out of the darkness into shadows flecked with

white, like snow, that gathered into a blinding, glaring whiteness.

"Callie!" Liss whimpered, holding fast with both hands. "O-oh, man! Keep ahold. I can't see you, it's so bright."

They stood on a bright hill in a spring dawn. It seemed a brighter sun, a bluer sky, an earth greener than they had dreamed; but still there was a whiteness, a graininess in the air that faintly blurred and bleached this crystal world and softened all its sounds.

The grass they stood in rustled about their knees. Here was no wood, but a long, grassy hilltop, an island in a forest sea. On all sides the hill fell away to meet the climbing trees. These were giants: broad butternuts, spreading oaks with new leaves paling to a silvery white, tulip trees springing straight and tall, their waxy flowers like cups to catch and hold the early sunshine. There were sweet gum trees, and here and there a large-leafed pawpaw glowed with dark winey flowers that touched the warm air with an odor like ripe grapes. Crab apples early in full bloom glowed white in the green wood, blowing the wild sweet fragrance of apples upward through the grass. In the forest valley far below, a river wound, and in the middle of its broadest reach an island stood, green and white with giant sycamores and flowering apples.

Callie looked at Liss, and Liss at Callie. For all the strangeness, the wildness, and pale brilliance, they knew where they were. The shape of the hills, the bones of the earth, were not changed, even though it seemed a different world. They stood on the Edge, on the crest of Apple Ridge. But though they knew the "where," neither found a voice to ask the why and how and when. In the look they exchanged, there was alarm and blame and unbelief. Who got who into this? The question was forgotten when a distant sound, a horn, broke their amazement into fear and curiosity.

The sound of singing came up from the forest: voices balanced in melody and harmony, moving upward toward them. There was sadness in the song, but its mode and measure held sweetness, too. The words were indistinguishable. The song ended with a bird call, a dawn-song rising on the breeze, as a large company of men, women, and children came from under the forest's eaves and into the waving grass. They were light-footed and slender folk, small, brown-skinned, and most of them dark-eyed. They wore simple robes and loincloths of woven stuff dyed golden brown or wine color or brilliant blue. At their head walked a young man, scarcely more than a boy, who wore a thin gold circlet around his brow. Immediately behind came a woman in blue, head bowed, holding to her breast a package wrapped in otterskin. A pendant hung at her neck: a disk of bronze with a design that flashed in silver. Their companions numbered several hundred. An old man among them, dressed in white, raised a chant. The attention paid him revealed him as a man of rank and authority.

"*Tlegúro e záral ir miríguin, num gualevóer!*" The words blurred together.

"They don't see us," Liss whispered, pointing where eight men carrying a litter were being directed to a mound of earth rising out of the grass a distance to the south. "How can they *not* see us?" Her voice was muffled, as if she spoke through cotton wool. She pushed her hood back.

"How'm I supposed to know? And hush up. Who *wants* them to see us?"

As they whispered, the woman in blue raised her head and looked about her distractedly, peering almost furtively at the grass, the trees behind, and upward along the brow of the hill. As Callie rubbed nervously at the blue-green stone in her pocket, the woman's eyes opened wide and fastened on her. She clasped the package more tightly to her breast and bit her lip as if to keep from crying out.

"Be careful," Callie hissed. "That one sees us. The woman in front."

Liss scanned the crowd as it fanned upward across the hillside. "Nobody else does, though. Do you s'pose we're invisible or something?" She faltered. "I don't like it. I want to be home."

"You tell me how, and I'm right behind you," Callie muttered. "I don't like it one little bit either. You know what this is? This is a funeral we've plonked into." Reluctantly, she felt her gaze drawn back to the woman in blue. She was watching the girls avidly, as if she expected them to speak or make a sign.

"*Tlegúro e záral ir miríguin, num gualevóer,*" the old man intoned again. "Moon and morning star, enlighten us!"

Liss and Callie drew closer. From the moment the woman Erilla had seen them, their ears were sharpened and the mist was wiped from their vision. The hillsides flamed with a green dulled long ages since, and the forest with a growth and blossoming sadly diminished in later days. It was unreal, like walking in a vision, Liss thought, or a dream where you can understand the speech of birds, for they could understand these folk. The language was strange, but they could understand it. Callie knew the woman had something to do with it, but she held her tongue and let curiosity move her feet.

The bearers set the litter upon the grass. The old man took the young man by the hand, and together they knelt beside the body on the litter. From the ornament he wore in his long white hair, the elder took a blue feather and placed it on the forehead, and from a pouch at his side the younger took a polished blue-green stone and laid it on what must be his father's lips; for from the honor done them, it seemed the dead man had been the ruler of these people and that the younger now was king.

The woman—casting uneasy glances aside to where the girls stood hand in hand, fearful of moving—went to look down at her lord's face and then at the old man. She slipped the fur-wrapped package under a fold of her robe.

"I have nothing to send with him, Ayacas," she said, "except sweet memories. What else I have is for the living."

There was a murmur of approval from many in the crowd, but unease stirred many more. A dark man clad in white like Ayacas, but with a dyed yellow and orange border to his robe, pushed through the crowd. His eyes shone and his voice shrilled.

"And are we to be ruled by Erilla the Queen? May we not hear the voice of Amalahtis, the son of Tepollomis? Know this—" He stabbed a finger toward the queen. "Were Erilla truly filled with love for the living, she would follow Tepollomis, for the return of two souls to the Sun makes him shine more surely than one. If we must fear the spreading power of the kings of Cibotlán, it is because we deny the Sun his due. Are we become such barbarians in this age that we have forgotten how to sacrifice?"

"Hold your tongue, Neolin," Ayacas snapped. "You rant like a priest of Cibotlán, not a wise man of Abáloc. Let Amalahtis speak."

Amalahtis raised a hand. "I honor my mother, for she is the flower that blooms even in the snow. And yet I cannot keep from my heart a measure of dismay. Where have we gone wrong that we should dwindle so and be harried like rabbits before a pack of dogs? Sacrifice? No, that cannot be the answer, Neolin. Through it we would sacrifice all heart's ease for naught but secret fear, of which we have enough already. There is not one here among our brothers and sisters whom I would offer up in exchange for a strange god's smile."

He did not see the secret satisfaction that grew in Neolin's eyes.

"Yet I will do something," Amalahtis said, "to give my father honor, such as our neighbors gave their kings in the days of their greatness. By such honors to the past, Ayacas, may we not confirm his virtues in ourselves and strengthen our hearts?"

The old man hesitated. "Aye, my lord. At the least, I think it can do no harm. And if it strengthens you in your meeting with the future, why, that is good."

Amalahtis made a sign, and the crowd parted to let through a file of men carrying willow baskets. The first approached, bowed, and poured the contents of his basket over the litter where Tepollomis lay. The crowd sighed, impressed.

"It just looks like shiny gravel," Callie whispered. "Let's go see."

The passage into the mound was not yet roofed over, and as they watched, the litter was carried along its length and slid down into the round chamber at its end. Bearer after bearer entered, each adding his burden to the heap of tribute around and over the litter. There were copper bracelets, obsidian knives, carved stone pipes, sheets of silvery mica set into carved stone for mirrors, necklaces made of shells and nuggets of gold, and long strings of the shiny gravel.

"Why, it's *pearls!*" Liss gasped.

"And they're gonna *bury* it all?"

Something of the same dismay stirred the one called Neolin. Callie stood near enough to see the veins across his temples swell and to hear his teeth click, as if he bit back dangerous words. He turned and looked at her full in the face, and she felt in that stare all the venom of a serpentine mind. He peered behind him.

Callie turned away quickly, pulling Liss with her.

"What is it? Did he see you?"

"Yes . . . no! Oh, come away. He looked straight at us, and if he didn't see, he sure was looking."

They slipped along the fringes of the crowd, keeping their eyes down. Perhaps it was a two-way thing. If they singled out a person and looked too hard, perhaps then they could be seen themselves.

Amalahtis's voice rose in the chant, *Tlegúro e záral ir miríguin.* Then he gave commandment for the stones to be laid in place and the mound completed. "We shall build a great fortification here on the Field of Morning, to defend my father's resting place and to be a barrier against our enemies to the east and south and a watching place against those from the west."

"It is good. I think it is good." Ayacas nodded to himself.

"No!" Neolin leaped upon the half-completed mound. His glance darted over the crowd, searching. He raised his arms. "Not earthworks and palisading, but a temple! What help are the works of men when gods are thwarted? Better we should build a temple, a temple to house the oracle of the Serpent, and to raise Amalahtis and his priests nearer the Sun, his Brother." Turning, Neolin stretched out his arms to the sun climbing in the east and cried out in a chant that was half howl:

> "*Tonatiuh quautlevanitl*
> *Xippilli, nteutl*
> *Tone, tlaextia motonameyotia,*
> *Tontoqui, tetlati, tetkaati, teytoni, teixlileuh,*
> *Teixtlilo, teixcaputzo, teixtlecaleuh.*"

At the first jangling phrase the host on the hillside shrank together and murmured among themselves.

"They're asking what he's saying," Liss whispered. "They don't understand either."

"I'm not so sure *I* don't," Callie said uneasily, for as Neolin turned away from the sun, arms still raised, his gaze flickered over and around her like the lick of snakes' tongues. "How do we get out of here? Come on. This way."

She dragged Liss downward toward a great oak at the forest's edge, but Liss held back, fighting her, caught like all of the others in the spell of Neolin's words.

"Hear me!" Neolin cried. "For I speak with the voice of the Sun Serpent. Yestereve he came to me after midnight, here, in the darkness of the moon. The stars' lights were blown out, and a wind gathered around me, buffeting me with noise and coursing through me as a storm. I writhed, and my bones burned, for the Sun Serpent was within me, crying upon the hill with a great voice. 'Give, give,' he cried. 'I thirst, I thirst!' My flesh melted and my joints were as water, and he left me weeping upon this hilltop. 'Give!' If Erilla the Queen will not give herself as Sun Queens do, if Amalahtis will not spare one among us to be offered up, the god himself provides! Ei! See there the gifts he thirsts for! Behold in your midst strange maidens of the Sun and Moon!" His arm swung down, his finger stabbing through the air.

The crowd divided, shrinking apart, turning in astonishment to see two strange children, clad in outlandish and heavy garments, running for the shelter of the trees.

The coats and boots slowed them, or they would not have been caught so quickly. The folk swarmed after them, unthinking, spurred by Neolin's frenzy, and handed them back up the slope, touching them and exclaiming. Amalahtis stared, and Neolin scrambled down the loose earth face of the mound. Erilla made her way to her son's side.

"I saw them before." She marveled. "Are they not wonders?"

Unhearing, Amalahtis shook his head in amazement. "He conjured them. Neolin conjured them up in the Sun's name! If his power is so great, surely his wisdom is worth heeding."

Neolin hovered over the children, poking and exclaiming. Callie, even in her terror, noticed the sour and pungent smell of him, the stringiness of his oily black hair, the dirt grained in his knuckles. He ran a sharp-nailed finger down her cheek. Callie shivered and Liss squealed.

Erilla looked from her son to Neolin. "No! What you are thinking is evil! Children are for growing—for *bringing* the future, not for sacrifice as remedy to the past."

"But these are not our children. See how odd they are, how shy and strange. Like young birds." Neolin's voice was honey-smooth, but the children saw his eyes narrow with calculation. "Young cuckoos, I fear. Ah, it is the wise robin who breaks the egg the cuckoo lays among her pretty speckled ones. Young cuckoos grow up greedy and push the robins from the nest, my queen." His voice became a strangely distant chanting. "I, Neolin, hear wisdom crying out, 'Cage them! Cage them, or Abáloc will cease to be what it was and is, for they are bitter Birds of Change.' Wisdom tells Neolin the gods would have us send them to the kings of Cibotlán. If Abáloc is too tenderhearted to return them to the gods, Cibotlán will not be." His tone grew crafty. "And gifts to kings buy time and favor."

Those nearby had edged away from the girls. Only the queen did not shrink back, but she paled as Neolin smiled malevolently and watched her from the corners of his eyes.

"For growing?" he mused. "Yes, we shall have to fatten them with sugar and cakes." He pinched Callie's thin wrist.

She winced and closed her eyes, wishing it were a dream to wake from, wishing . . .

53

"Hey! What you think you're doin' there? You take your hands off my sister, you hear?"

Callie's eyes flew open.

Harry, blinking but belligerent, stood on the mound's slope.

5

Harry frowned. "You mean like they didn't see you until they wanted to? Or were made to?"

"Maybe if they forget about us, then we'll disappear back home." Liss spoke halfheartedly, picking at a splinter on the floor of their wicker prison. The afternoon was cool, but she had taken off her coat and was using it as a cushion.

"Fat chance." Callie leaned her forehead against one of the heavy willow crosspieces and peered out across the tidy patchwork of maize fields to the village. "What if we can't ever get back? Mama will be having fits already. It will be past suppertime at home."

"Yeah." Harry agreed sulkily. "And I'm hungry."

"O-o-oh, you're awful, Harry Rivers!" Liss glared at him, red-eyed. "If you followed us to help us, why aren't you thinking how to get us out, instead of worrying about your dumb stomach?"

"Who said I followed you? I was starting down the hill to phone home from old man Douglass's place when I got zapped here. It sure wasn't my idea."

"But you were worried about Callie," Liss persisted.

55

"Heck, no," he answered sullenly. "Old Cal can take care of herself."

Callie smothered a grin. "Unhand my sister, you villain," she intoned. She stood and shook her fist dramatically.

"Oh, come off it."

"*You* come off it. I was scared spitless, and I wished like heck to be home—and there you were, like a miracle or magic!"

"Don't you see?" Liss was excited. "Don't you suppose it's because you're twins? Twins are supposed to be more tuned in to each other, aren't they? And know when each other's in trouble. You *thought* him here, Callie."

Harry snorted. "Oh, sure. So now there are three of us in this birdcage instead of two. Thanks a bunch for thinking of me."

Liss sat back. "Well, I bet it *was* that." She sniffled and tried to pretend she hadn't. "If only there was somebody could wish us back the other way. I want to be home."

Callie examined their prison again. It was small—about five feet by ten—and shaped rather like a basket set up on four legs. It was even made like a basket, woven from willow branches as thick as a man's thumb; and there were skins stretched over the top to keep the weather out. At one end there was a door, and on one side two small hatches, placed above their reach, near the ceiling. All were hinged and fastened with leather thongs.

"This isn't really a jail, you guys." She dropped her voice to a whisper and pointed to a dry corncob wedged in one corner and to the kernels visible on the ground underneath the woven floor. "It's some kind of storage bin for corn. We could *chew* our way out, come dark. If we had a knife, we could be gone already."

"I got one." Harry fished in his coat pocket and then in his jeans, coming up with a clasp knife. "So what?"

56

"So *what?*" Liss grabbed it and fumbled at the large blade.

"Give it here. Your fingernails are too long." Callie pulled the blade out and moved to the door.

"Where you gonna run to?" Harry drawled. "You see down there by that far corn patch? That leetle man in the cute leetle basket like a cute little bus-stop shelter? He's been whacking his cute little paddles together to keep the birds off his seedlings. One yell and he'd have the whole bunch down here beating on us."

"Well, at least we'd be doing something," Liss snapped.

"Sure we would. Like a dog chasin' his tail."

Callie wavered. "But we might get away up to the hill."

Liss agreed. "The Field of Morning, they call it. And if we found the exact spot we came to, maybe we could get away home."

"With all those guys up there building their old fort? Besides, you say I came at a different place from where you did." He leaned back against the willow wall, stretching his legs, and tried to look cool and uncaring. "Why knock your head against it? Things could be worse. They could all be like that Neolin creep. If you ask me, I think I'm in a bad dream. Too much pie or something."

"You lump!" Callie flared out at him. "You're a mule, you are. Don't you *care?*"

"Not when I know I'm losin'."

Callie closed the knife slowly and slipped it into her own coat pocket.

"Aren't you hot?" Liss asked, looking up.

"No. Hey, look there." Callie pointed down the path that passed the corn shed. "They must be coming to take us out to dinner." She made a face.

Liss giggled shrilly, a little wildly. "It is a dream, isn't it?"

Harry bit his lip.

58

Ayacas led the children down into the village, courteously pointing out the storehouses, the bathhouse, and the council house as they went. Small children followed them at a distance, chattering and pointing, and women working in the fields and groves stood and stared. Folk along the street gave them a wide berth. The village itself was a pleasant place without apparent plan, with a wide avenue crossed here and there by lesser streets or paths. The lodges, willow-woven and covered with hides, were spaced out among the trees. Many sat in the middle of their own orchards. They passed fire circles, herb gardens, and pleasant groves and crossed a wide path curving down through massive sycamores to the riverbank. Bright birds, green parrot-like birds with yellow heads, wings touched with orange and yellow, darted through the cool shade in flocks and chattered in the boughs.

"Parrots?" Callie exclaimed.

Liss was lost in admiration of the flowers and sweet-scented trees. Where a small stream spilled down from the highlands above, dams had been constructed and pools fashioned, their banks lined with stones and moss and flowers.

"No, not parrots, exactly," Harry answered. "Cousins of, maybe. At least, they're not like the ones I've seen. You know, I guess this could be a kind of neat place to live, but if I'd been asked, I sure wouldn't want to visit."

"Ha, ha," Callie said unenthusiastically. "What do you suppose they call this place?"

Ayacas had walked ahead. Now he stopped and regarded them with amazement. "You speak strangely indeed for emissaries of the gods. How is it that you do not know that you are in Abáloc?"

"Apple Lock?" Harry's head jerked up. "What did you say, man?"

The girls stood, speechless.

"No." Ayacas spoke cautiously, doubtfully, as if alarmed by their reaction. "Not Abbalok, Abáloc."

"You guys hear that? Abáloc!" Harry's listlessness disappeared. "How could a name stick as long as . . . as however long it's been? I thought the place was named Apple Lock for all the crab-apple trees and for that big river-lock downstream." He looked around him at the lay of the ground and downslope to the river. "How creepy can you get? I bet we're walking through the courthouse or Weebles' store right here."

The men following behind exchanged puzzled looks with old Ayacas.

"I do not understand either," the old man said, in some confusion. "Where . . . Do you come from the spirit realm or from . . . some other place? I know of no country where folk are so pale or so dark as you."

"We're from here. From Apple Lock," Harry answered. "From here."

The old man showed alarm and concern. Then, turning, he bustled on ahead.

"How *about* that?" Harry marveled. "Do you suppose if we get stuck here, we get erased back home in the future, or what?"

"Great gumboots!" Liss laughed despite her nervousness. "You're a nut, you know?"

"Amen," Callie pronounced with some acidity. "He can't be bothered to escape from the basket before he gets thrown in the soup. Oh, no. But you give him a puzzle-game, and he worries it like a dog with a boney-bone. OK, smart-face. What's the answer? Or don't you know?"

Harry pulled at his lip and screwed up his eyes in concentration. "We got here in our own clothes, didn't we? Now, if we'd been all gunched up in blue robes or bath towels with pearls all over, there'd be something to worry about. The real problem is: *if* we get home, *when* will we get home? Before we left or five years later? You remember that report Hagedorn gave in science class about space travel, and how they figure there's something weird in the timing? You get back, and you're younger. I mean, everybody else has gotten old faster."

"I think if you've got some other riddle in your noodle, we'd like it better," said Callie as they came to the entrance of the king's lodge.

It was larger than the other dwellings, but smaller by far than the council lodge. The skins along the walls had been rolled up and fastened. Amalahtis and Erilla waited in the doorway, and Ayacas behind them. The young man was flushed, and a slight arrogance in his manner showed that he was ill at ease.

"Amalahtis the King apologizes for himself and for all the remnant of his people," he said with a stiff bow. "It was wrong of us to imprison you so hastily. Neolin's zeal overrode both his judgment and my own. Ayacas and my mother Erilla say you may in some strange fashion be friends or kindred to us, and we would have you enter and sup with us."

"More, we would have you explain certain riddles to us," said Erilla. Her dark eyes danced with excitement.

"Hold!"

An angry Neolin came bustling up the path, followed by two stout young men. He glared from Ayacas to the children.

"I was bringing guards to the granary when I heard of this foolishness. Why are their arms not bound? And why are they here? It is not good to have converse with those who are . . . set apart. So the wisdom of Abáloc tells us."

"Does it, Ayacas?" the queen asked. She fixed the older man with a stern look he tried in vain to evade.

"So it may, my lady," was his evasive answer. "Certainly

I have heard such a saying before. It may be that the wise man guards against the silver tongue of his captive, lest he be enslaved by him in turn. But," he ventured, "I do not think that can apply in this case."

Neolin flared. "How can you say so? You, too, learned your lore at my grandfather's feet, old man. Have you forgotten the precept, 'A man's heart is best filled with his own kind'?"

"I have not forgotten it. Yet I would be hard put to know where are the bounds of kindred." Blandly, he asked, "Your own mother was of an unknown people far to the west, was she not?"

Neolin drew his breath in with a hiss, and when he answered, it was with a dangerous sweetness.

"Yes, old man. Unknown. Unknown, but not unlike. These are . . . different. And the weakling people that opens its gates and hearts to strangeness ends with broken gates and trampled hearts, and the face it sees in the mirror is the stranger's. Not so Cibotlán. Cibotlán knows how to feed its power."

"Or is it that the strong are only *thought* strong?" countered old Ayacas. "May it not be knowledge that the heart of Cibotlán is hollow? May it not be fear itself that drives the Seven Kings to walk upon the necks of those who will not adopt their ways?"

The younger man sneered. "Does great Cibotlán then fear *our* puny strength? I had not thought Abáloc so potent."

Ayacas folded his arms and spoke reprovingly. "No, not as you mean. But neither do you fear bodily harm from children. Yet you seem to say we should fear these three. Riddle me that."

Amalahtis waved an impatient hand, brushing aside what was sure to become a bitter squabble. "No, Neolin. It will not do. We are not Cibotlán. We need no power over

62

others, nor wish it." His voice trembled between anger and doubt. "If to buy time and favor you would send these children to our enemies, perhaps another time you would have us send our own? Wisdom? Wisdom should make life bloom. How can it do so when it counsels violence and death? You bewilder me. This morning you would have had my mother join my father Tepollomis in death, saying it was most fitting! And now this. Are all wise men of two minds?"

Neolin's mouth snapped shut. Clearly, Amalahtis's firmness was a surprise to him, and not a pleasant one. He squinted, his face a mask of balked anger, and then schooled himself to a frigid courtesy.

"Very well, my lord. If I have offended, it is only through excess of love for my lord and my people. Tepollomis and his father-king before him let themselves be guided by the wise. But I will say no more. I trust we will not pay in death and tears for your kindness to these spirit-shapes, for surely you must see that they are not truly human?"

Amalahtis's face flamed. "Enough!"

Without another word Neolin bowed, turned, and stalked down the pathway to where a cloaked figure awaited him near the river road. After some hesitation, the two young men excused themselves and followed.

As the children were led into the house, Harry whispered, "Phew! But if they're not gonna eat *us*, I sure wish they'd bring on the food."

6

Their hosts seated themselves on a brightly colored rug that ran the length of the floor and bade the children do likewise. Three women quietly served a savory stew in wooden bowls and set out dishes and baskets of nuts and maple-sugar cakes. There were bowls, too, of a cherry-flavored drink, slightly bitter, but refreshing.

Erilla looked at them with open wonder. "Such moon-pale and earth-dark children! What are we to call you?"

Ayacas frowned at their answer. "Cali, Liss? Hari? Strange names."

"Strange names!" Amalahtis laughed. He was little more than a boy himself—perhaps eighteen, though it was hard to tell—and excitement and curiosity had already erased the uneasiness that had followed his clash with Neolin. He spread his arms wide. "My head spins with all I have heard prophesied and claimed and advised and denied this day. Tell me this: how is it that you speak our tongue and come among us claiming to be children of Abáloc? Your clothing is as strange as your skins, and you cannot deny that there was some wizardry in your coming."

64

"It wasn't our idea to come," Liss said quickly. "And we'd like to get back to our own Apple Lock, if you please."

"Back to?" Erilla looked at her intently. "How do you mean?"

"She means 'forward to,' " Harry explained. "I guess our Apple Lock is in the future now. What year is this?"

"What year?" Amalahtis looked blank. The question seemed to have no meaning to him, as if his mind could not conceive of the numbering of years.

Not so Ayacas. But the old man was wary. "That I should not tell you. How should children know of such a thing to ask it? The old calendar lore was reserved to the wise men, and even our knowledge has fallen into decay, until now only Neolin can read the stars. I am ignorant of such reckonings. Still, I have learned from him somewhat of the calendar of Cibotlán. By their count we are some hundred years and more into the second thousand years of the Fifth Sun."

"That's a big help." Harry rubbed at the bridge of his nose. "Still," he said, "I don't see how this could be the *future*. You all look kind of Indian-ish. But we might be a thousand years or more back."

Harry was doubtful. The folk of Abáloc were brown-skinned, with dark hair and eyes, and they carried themselves with the easy alertness of deer, but still they were unlike any of the Indians he had studied in fourth grade. Or seen. For one thing, they were neither tall, as he supposed old Chingachgook, the last of the Mohicans, must have been, or stocky, like John Ikkemotubbe down home in Daingerfield. Small and well-proportioned, with tiny feet and restless, expressive hands, these people dressed in rich colors that Harry thought no Indian hunter or woodsman would ever wear. They must somehow have been lost count of in the years between now and Apple Lock as he knew it. All this flicked through Harry's mind in the moment when

65

his eyes met those of Ayacas. The old man's eyes were a piercing blue, startling in a face as dark as old leather.

Liss shook her head violently. "The mounds! That's it. The ones at Moundsville and over at Mingo Junction are old as old. Ours must be, too."

"But, then . . . what are you saying? That you come from a time that has not yet happened?" Amalahtis was incredulous. "Such things are not possible. Are they?"

Callie had been staring at the pendant Erilla wore on a thong around her neck. It was of bronze, engraved, with silver inlaid in a simple pattern—a blossoming tree enclosed within a border.

"There! Liss and I saw that before." She tried to explain. "You see, on the hill up above our Apple Lock, we found a mound—a long heap about five, six feet high—and in one end we found this hole, you know? And a passageway down and in, kind of like the one you closed up this morning? And in the inside there was a pile of stuff. Like a cup made out of a pearly shell, and a gray-green stone bowl with two squirrels carved on the rim. And that—that medal. It happened while we were looking at that stuff. Whoosh! And here we were, and here you all were."

Erilla fingered the medallion. "There is no other like this," she said slowly. "It has come down to me, the . . . the last of the treasures of the City of the Moon under the Mountain. And I have such a cup and dish as you describe, also. My younger son, Lincoas, who was stolen away, gave the cup to me." A shadow crossed her face, and at her sign the women came to clear away the remains of the meal.

Ayacas clapped his hands together. "But then, this may be the best of luck! If you are from the future, you can tell us much. Will we be driven from this last corner of our dwindling kingdom? Shall we pay tribute to the kings of Cibotlán as they demand? Ah, there is so much that you can tell us."

66

Harry was uncomfortable. He shrugged. "We never even heard of you."

Liss nodded. "Nobody did. My grandfather's grandfather came to—*will* have come to Apple Lock over a hundred and fifty years before our time, and there wasn't even an Indian village here. Most people nowadays don't know about all the old mounds *being* up and down the river."

"The ancestors of our neighbors built many of them," Amalahtis explained. "But now many are fled, and their villages stand empty. Those who remain made Sun temples, and pay tribute to the Seven Kings of Cibotlán. Cibotlán spreads like a plague across the land. They are the locusts and we the harvest."

"You should write all about your people; write it down in a book and stick it in one of your mounds," Liss said enthusiastically. "Then when we get home, we can find it and tell everybody. If we could read it, I mean." It occurred to her that would be small consolation to these folk, and to cover her clumsiness, she asked, "How do we understand you now? Is it magic? Or some kind of telepathy?"

"I do not know what that may be." Erilla smiled. "But it seems that though my ears hear you speak in strange sounds, in my mind it is as if you spoke the tongue of Abáloc."

Amalahtis interrupted. "What is this thing called 'book'? And what is 'write'?"

The children looked at him blankly, and then at Ayacas, who was strongly agitated. Only Erilla seemed unmoved.

"Why, *writing*. Keeping records. You know, making marks that stand for words," Liss insisted.

"We have no such skill."

"Stop, stop!" Ayacas waved his hands nervously. "These things must not be spoken of. Such making of signs is forbidden. What the gods will have us know of the past is in the hands of the wise men. The gods took the magic signs away because they fed men's pride more than their wisdom." He stood rubbing his hands nervously, as if he wished to bring the conversation to an end.

"Don't flip," Harry said rudely, alarmed that Liss might have stirred up something dangerous. "Who needs books? All we need is to get home. That's *our* problem, and we haven't got anything to do with yours. No*how*."

"Perhaps not. Perhaps not." Ayacas fussed. "But come, my lord. We must find Neolin, to placate his anger. He may be rash, but he has much useful learning, knowledge that his grandfather would not impart to me. If these folk have knowledge of the old skill of making the magic symbols, they may also have some other power we should fear." The old man wavered. "Neolin should hear what these children say before we talk further."

Amalahtis hesitated, but then hurried after him down the path through the trees.

"Not meaning to be rude," Callie said after a silence, "but I get the idea nobody around here knows what end is up. All I can say is, if you got a war on, how come you didn't lose it already? What good's a wise man who doesn't even know his own mind?"

Erilla smiled faintly. "Neolin has them confused. You see, Ayacas, as the elder, should have been the one to learn the mysteries: the music of life, the lore of herbs, the sagas of the kings, the wisdom of Abáloc. But Neolin, when he had returned to us from among his mother's people, persuaded his grandfather, our last sage, to leave off teaching Ayacas and to give him the greater wisdom instead. At times I have thought that what Neolin says is different from what our parents heard from earlier sages, but I cannot be sure. And Neolin will not teach the young. He is jealous with his wisdom. Once we followed game and the forest's plenty with light hearts and never hungered. Then as we lost our own traditions, we took what seemed to us good from our neighbors—the planting of maize, a song or hero tale, or a healing herb we had not known. But now Cibotlán would have us bow our necks and take on the full burden of their ways. It is a heavy burden indeed, for they demand a tithe of children as 'food for the Sun.' "

Erilla turned to stare out across the green and flowering lawns. "Tepollomis, my husband-king, was on a hunting and gathering trip with our second son, Lincoas, and other young men and women when he met his death. The men of the lord Tulal of Cibotlán fell upon them and took Lincoas and the others captive. We shall not see them again, and they were the greatest part of our hope." She turned back angrily. "These are the ways Neolin would bring us to! And none has knowledge or authority to call his counsel evil."

"How come people just don't up and tell him off?"

"Habit. Habit," she said wearily. "And the fear of losing the lore of medicine and the stars, which no other knows." She lowered her voice. "But now that you are here, claiming knowledge of books, it may be that you have come to free us. Look here."

Moving a basket that stood in the corner, she lifted the carpet and scooped away sand to reveal the otterskin package she had carried that morning. She unwrapped it.

"I had meant to bury this with Tepollomis. You see, once our folk had many books. It was not until the day of my grandmother's grandmother, a time of many disasters, that an oracle bade us leave our old home and abandon our books. We were no longer to teach our children the meaning of these marks."

She held out a book to Harry. He took it reluctantly, but was interested in spite of his determination not to be drawn. It was a beautiful thing, with polished plaques of rose crystal for covers and a clasp of a pale metal something like gold. On the first page, written carefully in inks of brown and red and blue, were these signs:

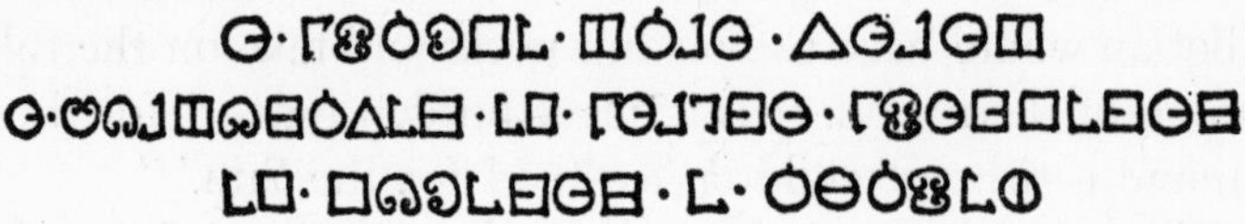

Harry shrugged. "I never saw anything like it." He passed the book to Callie. Liss leaned over Callie's shoulder to see.

"It looks more like decorations than writing," Liss said. "Is each sign a word?"

Callie ran her finger over the page. "It's great! You got a pencil, Harry? I think I've got a piece of paper here somewhere." She fumbled in a coat pocket. Harry handed her a stub of a pencil and a small, dog-eared notebook. She began copying the figures onto a clean page. "They're pretty—like a design for on something."

Erilla looked from one to the other of them in dismay. "You cannot read it? But you must! How else are we to recover the past, to struggle against the chaos of forgetfulness? How else can we pass on our lore? Cibotlán will surround and swallow us. Except for Neolin," she said bitterly. "And I had hoped the book might tell where our ancient city under the mountain lay." She spoke wistfully. "We could go there. I remember my grandmother's tales of its beauty, which she heard from her grandmother. It lies far from here, I think. Far from the cities of Cibotlán."

"How come you have the book at all?" Liss was curious.

"Ah, you see, my grandmother's grandmother mistrusted oracles. She could not read herself, but she saved and hid this one book, the *Book of the Kings of Abáloc*. And it was passed down from daughter to daughter's daughter, a dark secret. A dark secret." She laughed ruefully. "And I've no daughter. So there's an end to it." Catching sight of her son and Ayacas at the foot of the path, she retrieved the book, wrapped it hastily, and concealed it in a basket at her side.

Callie scrawled quickly on the lined page: *Book of the Kings of Abálock.*

"But that's in English," Liss whispered. "You've got to write how it sounds in Abalockian."

"Oh, gory bibduddle!" Callie screwed her eyes tight, trying to sort out sound and meaning.

"*E plévro or Rigóues o Abáloc.*" Erilla spoke the words slowly, in a low voice, giving them the faintly old-fashioned pronunciation she remembered from her childhood when she had first seen the book and heard its whispered name. A new doubt made her voice falter. "But what good does it do to write in your strange shapes if you do not know which of our signs is which?"

Callie, concentrating hard on the sounds, wrote: A PLEVROW OR REGOOWAYS O ABALOCK. Harry snatched the notebook from her as she finished and stuffed it in his inside coat pocket.

Amalahtis and Ayacas were apologetic. Neolin was nowhere to be found, and they had returned, still undecided what was best to do. A small boy in the village claimed to have seen the priest hurrying through the dusk toward the pass behind the south hill in company with a stranger, a man hooded and cloaked. But the tale was unlikely, and they had not wished to chance sending a runner after a rumor. It would be as well to wait until the morrow for decisions. By Amalahtis's orders, a pleasant lodge nearby and beds—pallets filled with sweet-smelling grasses—were provided for the children. They were given blankets and thin pillows and bid a kind but vague good night.

"Hoo!" Harry exclaimed. "I get the feeling we oughta tuck *them* in."

"They're nice," Liss protested. "Only think how great a place this would be if only they weren't so . . . lost."

"Anybody who's dumb enough to throw away his compass deserves to get lost." Harry was bored again.

"Not lost." Callie was thoughtful. "Turned around. They're all turned around. On purpose, I bet. On somebody's purpose. I wonder where that creepy what's-his-name went."

"Well, it looks like we've thrown *our* compass away and didn't know it," Liss said.

Callie screwed her eyes shut. "Something. There's something about that creep, that Neolin. . . . All that junk about how they should be scared of us? *He* didn't believe it."

Harry propped himself up on an elbow. "Man, he's so cool, he's a walking icicle. He had 'em jumping through hoops—'These are no children, my people; these are nasty insects. Our next-door neighbors have a big bug-bomb, so let's shoo 'em over there.'"

"But *why?*" Liss said, puzzled.

"I tell you what I think," Callie said darkly. "I think he wasn't really so awfully surprised to see us. He's just rattled because we came *here*, to Abáloc. I think we were expected, but somewhere else. *That's* what I think."

Harry stared and then snorted. "Lo, the brilliant female brain! A widdle bird told 'oo dat 'oo go'ed down d' wong hole, behaps?"

"Oh, shut up!" Callie rolled over and gave him a half-hearted clout with her pillow. She refused to say any more about her hunch. If only that Neolin had not said *Seven Kings*. . . .

They talked themselves out at last and were asleep even before it was fully dark.

The moon was high and the village slumbering when a slight sound roused Harry. Before he could sit up, a hand clapped over his mouth and strong arms held him fast. At the sight of the frightened girls being bound and gagged, he wriggled wildly, almost breaking free. As he struggled, a foul-tasting liquid was forced down his throat, and after a moment's thrashing about, he slid into unresisting sleep. Three carrying hammocks were brought, and a shadowy column of runners sped southward under the moon-dappled trees.

7

Liss was cold and angry. Her coat had been lost in the scuffle because she had been using it as an extra blanket instead of wearing it. The gag, a soft roll of cloth tied in place with a narrower strip, was not unbearably tight, but it was dry against her tongue, and she could not work up the spit to swallow. She needed desperately to swallow. The swaying of the net was worse than riding in the back seat of a car on a winding road. Because of the way the cloth pressed on her tongue, she could not squeal, but she could and did roar—a fierce, rough little animal sound pushing up to the back of her throat. It made her throat more dry and swallowing even more impossible. That made her angrier yet, and so she roared again.

The men laughed and called something forward up the line. They had been traveling at a fast pace for well over an hour and obviously thought themselves safely away from any who might hinder them, for they no longer took care to be quiet.

A command was passed back the line in answer, and

immediately the bearers lowered their burdens to the ground. In the faint moonlight that fell through a break in the foliage overhead, Liss sat up and watched a tall figure stride back along the trail. She was last in the line. He uncovered his shrouded lantern and stared at her so coldly that she could manage only a small rumble and an indignant wriggle. He spoke briefly to the bearers, turned, and walked away. Furious, Liss gathered up her breath to roar again as best as she could, but at just that moment one of the men slipped the knot loose on the gag and another untied her hands. The roar burst out, a surprised bellow echoing among the trees. She nearly choked on it, both for chagrin and for pain because it hurt. Someone thrust a blanket at her, and she took it gratefully.

"Listen to the poor wounded buffalo back there!" Callie's voice floated back, a little shaky. They had loosed her, too.

"Is Harry OK?" Liss called. He had looked so limp when they rolled him into the net and picked it up with the long carrying pole.

"I dunno. That stuff they gave him . . . I dunno." Liss could hear the worry in her voice.

"*Tzolát!* Silence!" The harsh word speared the darkness, and with it the bearers lifted the hammocks to shoulder height and sped along the trail.

At some time during the night, which seemed much longer than it should have been, a new team of bearers had come alongside, paced a moment, and taken the poles, moving on without a break in stride. By morning they had covered a considerable distance, and in the first half-light Liss could see that they still traveled south. The river gleamed dully, a leaden color, through the shadow trees.

Harry was awake. At intervals Liss had heard Callie calling, "Harry? You awake? You answer me, hear? I don't like seeing you swing up there like some dead fly in an old

75

spider web, you hear?" He must have made some sort of answer at last because her tone changed. "Bless poor weevils and dirty birds! What are *you* groaning about? You got some sleep, which is more'n we did."

The officer with this second relay of bearers made no objection to their talking, but he neither spoke to them nor allowed his men to. After a few guesses at how far they had come in the night, the girls, too, fell silent. Harry's head ached fiercely.

With the dawn itself, they came out of the forest onto a hillside only lightly wooded, where hedgerows of young trees divided garden plots of young maize, sweet potato, and tomato plants. Beyond, rising up out of the morning haze that hung above the river, was a gleaming city. It was unexpected, unbelievable, beautiful. On the valley floor, rolling hillocks stretched down toward the valley stream and the great river, falling away steeply into swampy green marshlands. In the middle distance, a great golden temple rose up into the morning, crowning a great mound that was circled by a broad moat. Two causeways crossed the moat, meeting wide, tree-lined streets that stretched west and east to the river and the rolling hills. Another, broader stone causeway carried the western road across the swamp to the river's edge, where small boats clustered along the pier. Within the palisaded walls of the inner city, there were lesser mounds, some bare except for a velvet carpet of grass and flowers, and others where stone stairs led up to shrines. Beyond the earthworks a maze of streets lined with smaller wooden buildings and tidy gardens stretched out in all directions. Smoke from morning fires rose from many houses, and drums beat a welcome to the dawn. After its first rosy glow, the children could see that the great temple itself was built of wood, but it was polished wood and richly carved.

76

The bearers ran steadily.

Fully awake at last, Harry wrestled around in the mesh hammock, trying to sit up. "Where the heck are we?"

Callie herself was speechless.

Liss swallowed. The dream feeling was back. She squinted her eyes shut, pressing her fingers against them, and then opened them quickly, as if she hoped it had been a mirage. But the tall mound sat there, unspeakably beautiful and horribly familiar.

"It's . . . it's Moundsville. All this? Callie, it's Moundsville!" she called shakily. "I've been here. It's Moundsville."

Callie lay back in the net. "How do you mean, you've been here?" She spoke carefully. At this point nothing seemed impossible, but it did seem most improbable that there could be such a place as this. "You mean, at home it's still here?"

"It *will* be still here, if we get home. Hardly any of it, though." She giggled nervously. "That big old mound is a block away from the State Penitentiary. My aunt and uncle drove the Drip and me down to see it summer before last. But nobody ever said it once was like this!"

"I bet you wish you'd brung your camera." Harry made a halfhearted attempt at sarcasm. He was too worried to pursue it. Even if by some incredible dumb luck they managed to escape, how could they make it back to Abáloc with no food and half the countryside after them?

They did not, after all, go down into the city of the Lord Tulal—for it was his, and the northwesternmost of the seven cities—but kept to the east and halted at a way station where their trail crossed the East Road. The children were taken into the house, a plain one-roomed shelter with benches around the walls and a fire pit in the center of the floor. There they were fed baked corn cakes and bowls of

77

hot, soft corn mush flavored with honey. For drink they had cups of water.

"What, no orange juice?" Harry asked, raising his eyebrows and throwing his head back.

Callie glared at him. If Harry got going on one of his ornery streaks, there was no telling what he might do.

But Liss grinned. "Or coffee. With cream."

"And two lumps." Harry flapped a hand toward the two stolid figures at the door. "The local fuzz can have the lumps."

The guards were dark, solid, stocky men, lightly clad and tattooed. Like the bearers who had seemed so alarming in the first daylight, each wore a distinctive design on one cheek and decorative bands around his arms and legs.

The children were silenced by the appearance of two other figures at the door. Neolin stood there with the cloaked and hooded man of the evening before. Neolin smiled, shaking his stringy locks.

"Are they not just as I said, Helhuac? There can be no doubt it is these the kings have watched for. And they fell into my hands like ripe fruit. The kings should be grateful indeed for such a gift from their faithful friend."

"Yes, yes. Yet the word from the east was that there were but two, a chalky boy and a black girl. I mislike it. If you are fool enough to court favor with a trick Neolin . . ."

"Nonsense! Feel their skins. See their faces. It is no trick of dyes or putties! See? Would I risk losing the confidence of both Abáloc and Cibotlán? The kings know me for their friend."

The other spoke abruptly and with a hint of contempt. "Very well. And here is their gratitude." He emptied a small pouch of gold nuggets into Neolin's hands.

"But . . ." The wise man of Abáloc seemed dismayed. "I had not meant . . . *this*, but some recognition, some support in my work in Abáloc."

The response was as cold as the voice was sharp. "Do you question the kings then?"

"No, no. Never that, my lord. Well, ah, I must be going. It is likely that I have been missed already." Neolin backed away and disappeared from view.

The cloaked man watched him away and, turning to the officer, said, "The man is a fool. He thinks to be king in Abáloc—king and priest, like the lord Quanohtsín himself." He turned to look at the children. "The more fool he to think we did not expect our young guests. Our honored guests. Come! Are the litters ready?" He disappeared with the officer.

"Now, what's *that* supposed to mean?" Liss whispered.

Traveling east and south from the city, the children found themselves more comfortably provided for. They rode in litters that were light in weight but had backs and armrests, cushions, and a sort of canopy that could be drawn at night. As before, the bearers were relieved at three-hour intervals, and they moved at considerable speed. The only discomfort came from the danger of falling off. Despite the skill of each team of four bearers, this was a complication they had not needed to worry about in the uncomfortable two-man sling hammocks. They soon learned the rhythm of balance and the importance of not shifting weight except with care.

There was no stop at midday. For a lunch, the officer who joined them with the new relay passed up corn cakes and cups of maple-sugar water. The hills became higher and more rugged as they traveled farther. In late afternoon they climbed, with some slowing of the pace, a mile-long river gorge where the water fell to meet them down a series of falls and rapids. Liss and Callie and Harry were too hungry and too stiff from the juggling and careful balancing to appreciate the rushing water and flowery banks. Bending at last away from the stream, the caravan turned due south and came to the banks of another small river or the same stream swinging back across their path. A small house of stone and timber nearby proved to be another way station, where the children were put down and given a supper of corn cakes, squash, sweet potatoes in a pie, and roast venison.

"That's more like it," Harry said, wiping his mouth on the back of his hand.

"I need a run around the block." Liss wheezed exaggeratedly.

"Maybe we all do." Callie snatched at the idea. "D'you suppose they'd let us walk for a while?" On their own feet they might have a chance to slip away into the heavy undergrowth in the dusk.

To their surprise, the officer made no objection, but he took the precaution of placing four of his men between each of them. With the leaders and rear guard, this effectively dampened Callie's vision of artful escape. They crossed the stream, which the men called Pochuanón, on a light bridge near the outpost and moved on at a pace that slowly increased to a jog. When the children were taken up again, the men bound blankets around the litters so that they could sleep without fear of falling.

At dawn they found themselves in a rugged mountainous area, passing below a massive eroded rock formation that looked more like a gigantic and crumbling castle from a dream than a mountain cliff. They breakfasted in a cave a few miles farther along the trail and during the day traversed ridges and valleys where distant ridges paled to a hazy blue that was an echo to the sky. At midday they passed a way station lodged in another cavern and were told that there were many caverns in this country, some large and very beautiful.

The children exchanged worried glances. What if one of these were the place of the Moon under the Mountain, the long-ago home of Abáloc, now surrounded by the far-reaching power of Cibotlán?

"Then that sinks that," Harry said. "Big surprise. Did you ever know a cookie to crumble any other way?"

"Oh, dry up." The girls spoke together.

The bearers looked perplexed, and Liss idly wondered whether they understood anything of what the children spoke among themselves, or if it were only that the slanging confused them. It seemed a good question, perhaps a useful one; and the children spent an enjoyable part of the afternoon running tests, but with contradictory results. Liss speculated that it might be, rather, the unfamiliar attitudes and things understood-but-left-unsaid that mystified them.

The trip became almost a pleasure. Its routine was reassuring, and they were treated with consideration, so it was easy to forget that they were captives. Perhaps they weren't, exactly. The man had said "honored guests," hadn't he? And for now, the mountains were beautiful—beyond each ridge another, richly green with a great variety of thick-trunked ancient trees. Dogwood and redbuds bloomed in the valleys and on the lower slopes. Azaleas were everywhere, and violets underfoot. Supper and nightfall came too soon. The longer the journey the better, the children told themselves. All the more time to get zapped back home—somehow.

Before dawn, in the descent from the high country, the procession crossed a river with a strange, harsh name—Tlapahuanóctl—and came to another way station.

"Tlapa—we'll never remember that." Liss yawned over her breakfast. "Even if we can figure out how to get forward in time, how'll we ever get back home from wherever we are, wherever that is?"

"Come again," said Callie.

Harry pointed toward the first faint glow of sunrise. "We've been heading straight east for a good while."

"East? Well, we've got Aunt Loretta in Baltimore." Callie bit into a corn cake. "If we land there, we're set."

"Yish!" said Harry.

Liss made a comical face. "And I've got an uncle in Washington. Anybody know anybody in . . . Richmond, Virginia?"

At full sunrise they saw the city in the distance: a great, glowing city stretched out below the fiery sun. With new runners the little procession was soon moving at a swaying trot across the wide meadows to its walls. They came through massive square-arched wooden gates and down a wide avenue lined with magnolias and cherry trees. At its end bulked a long, grassy mound with a broad stair up its middle, mounting to the largest of the three temples that stood above. Warriors lined the stair on both sides and dipped their spears as an official in a feathered headdress conducted the children up the steep steps.

At the top they were blinded by the sun glaring through the massive columned temple. A voice intoned, "Bow down to the Sun's Brother and his Brother Suns, the great lords Quanohtsín, Ititlán, Malinl, the lords T'zomoc and Tulal, Setsek and Lopan!"

Callie rubbed her dazzled eyes and saw the seven lords, dark shapes, some thin and tall, some shorter, approach them from within the silhouetted temple. Her knees felt weak as water, and Liss, half sensing her thought, shrank close to her.

Harry folded his arms and rocked gently on the balls of his feet, waiting. He was frightened, but ignored a second and third command to bow. The girls followed his example, and the official retired hastily, in fear and confusion.

The seven figures clad in white—faces, arms, and legs tattooed like richly colored tapestry, crowned with feathers of the paroquet and bearing willow rods—stepped out from the temple's shadow.

Callie knew them: the seven snowmen.

8

"Yes, Sun's Daughter," Quanohtsín answered Callie. "Our gods call across time for sacrifice, and those whose souls are heir to our own answer and perform it. The bloodless child who offered a rabbit on our altar drew us, and you gave us shapes to move in your world while we slumbered in this temple, bound in visions. We marveled at what we saw, and we wished you here, though it is strange that you should have come to Abáloc and not to us. Perhaps we were mistaken in you. But the small boy-child . . ."

"Never mind him. Why do you want my sister?" Harry demanded belligerently. "She never did anything to you."

Ititlán spoke smoothly, darting a warning look at his brother-kings. "No, no, young warrior. You misread my brother's meaning, but then half his talk is riddles. Still, you yourself are the answer to a riddle. There is in the tongue of our brothers from Aztlán a hymn of the sun which says:

" 'The eagle Sun, fire arrow,
    Year's ruler, Power,
Illumines his own with the blessing of his beams,
    Warms, burns, blackens them,
Makes dark their faces, black smoke to rise to Him.'

"Neither Aztlán nor Cibotlán have known the beauty of such folk as your sister and yourself. Yours are the faces of the old hymn. We wished to have her among us so that we might honor one of those most honored by the Sun. We are doubly glad that you have joined her. It is a double honor."

Harry, bewildered, relaxed a little. He did not quite know how to answer. What do you say, he wondered, when a guy you thought was going to bust you one starts bowing like you were a VIP visitor from another planet? Still, he could not ignore a tingling in the hairs at the nape of his neck. There was something else—something hidden, something nasty—even though the words were sweet and gratifying.

Quanohtsín commanded, and slaves brought cloaks of tapestry woven with feathers. One was moon-colored, silvery-gray and white, and that was given to Liss. The others were yellow and orange and red, blazoned with designs in purple and green.

"Keep it," Harry said stoutly. "I'm not gonna take my coat off. I'll need it when I get home." But he, and Callie, too, agreed to wear the cloaks over their coats. The morning was still young and cool.

Liss caught her breath at the sight of them. The effect was beautiful. They were dark Sun Birds, all warmth and glow and aliveness. Callie wore her stubborn look, chin up, and Harry walked as insolently as any king. They were led ahead of her through the colonnaded temple and out to the eastern rim of the flat-topped mound. Liss found herself at one side, flanked by guards, but was too caught up in the spectacle to notice how carefully they watched her.

A roar rose up to greet the kings and children. It shook the air like thunder. The avenue and fields below stretched a hundred yards or more to the banks of a broad river, and the wide expanse was crowded with many thousands of people. Those in the forefront were divided into companies, wedges of green and red and purple. Tattoos, feathers, and brightly dyed fringed cloths together made a kaleidoscopic shimmer. In the center, at the foot of the stair, was a splendid group. They were clad in blue garments heavy with embroidery of gold beads and pearls. The maidens were garlanded with flowers, and the young men wore feather headdresses shaped like peacocks' tails. The young man at their center wore a white tunic crusted with pearls, a cloak of gleaming white feathers, and an imposing headdress of egret plumes. And all the while the crowd roared, he played unheard upon a flute. His eyes were closed, and he and his companions swayed to the mounting chant.

"Eagle Sun, fire arrow,
Illumine us!"

Liss wondered who they were. Their skins were brown and unmarked, not like these others. Looking from the crowd to the soldiers and officials, and to the kings, she guessed that the more important these people were, the more decoration was allowed them. Some women and girl-children in the crowd had only a simple design pricked upon their foreheads, while the kings were covered, face and body, with writhing, sinuous designs and curious patterns. Like walking Oriental rugs, Liss thought, beautiful, but unhuman. As if their bodies and faces were something to be denied. The faces were worst. There was no way to read a frown or smile, pity or contempt, on those mobile masks of swirling color.

"Ya-hai!" Quanohtsín raised his hand, and the great chant died away like a reverberating organ note. "Suns and Lowly Ones of the City Quaunatilcó, peace!" His voice had a compelling, deep music. "The dark children are come among us as we begin preparations for the feast of him whose face is shining smoke. There could be no more favorable omen for the coming year than this, for though in our vision we saw the Sun Maiden, behold! She brings with her a brother to be the Chosen One!"

"Hey now, just a minute . . ."

Liss saw Callie and Harry draw together. She could feel the trembling excitement in the men who stood beside her, and she moved to get away, to get to Callie and Harry. But rough hands stopped her and tied her hands behind her back. She was terribly afraid but managed to keep quiet, in hopes that they would not take her away. It was not her they wanted. It was Sonny. The kings said they had dreamed of the Drip. And he . . . he had dreamed of voices calling him . . .

Harry eyed all around him suspiciously. "What do you have to do to be this Chosen-One thing?"

"Do? It is we who do for you, Sun Child." Ititlán bowed. "You shall come to the city of Tushcloshán, a city greater than this, and at the feast all of Cibotlán shall honor and worship you. Fine foods, precious robes, slaves, music, and flowers—and power—all these shall be yours."

Callie nudged and whispered. A little reluctantly, Harry pointed to Liss and asked, "What about her?"

"That need not concern you," said the one called Setsek sharply. An answer and no answer. Callie watched Liss furtively.

Harry stared at the soldiers, the crowd, the waiting kings. The sharpness of Setsek's reply, the moment's concern for Melissa; these stung him awake. The scene was as strange and shifting as any dream, but he was awake. The crowd waited, eager, hungry almost. The eyes of the terrible kings glittered in faces invisible behind tattooed medallions and foliage of red, green, blue, and purple. Their promises were good enough—shows, and eats, and music—but Harry was nervous about the sharp black eyes that peered out through stippled green and purple leaves and tendrils—like snakes in the grass.

"Maybe not," Harry said. "But she's with us, and she's gonna stay with us, I guess." He didn't really like Melissa, he remembered. Why did he stick his neck out for her? As his mind slid back to himself, the kings seemed warmer, smaller, less terrifying. "Besides, there's a hooker. There's gotta be a hooker." Harry looked more and more as if he hoped there weren't one. "A catch. You know—something nasty in the woodwork."

Their perplexity increased until T'zomoc, a short man and fatter than the others, suddenly laughed and said, "A condition. The Sun Child does not believe that the bear may reach the honey without being stung."

"Yeah, that's it." Harry frowned at the hint of grimness in their laughter.

"Then we must reassure him." Setsek smiled. He whispered to the others, and they nodded. The crowd below watched and waited docilely.

Quanohtsín stood forward to speak for the seven. "One thing you may do for us. A great festival, such as that we prepare for, has need of many offerings to the Sun. We are well supplied for ourselves, but there is a nation we would tempt into alliance with us, by providing an offering gift. The bloodless child—the Moon Child. If you bring him to us, Cibotlán will do you double reverence." He watched Harry through narrowed eyes. "It is but a small thing."

The Drip again. Why would they want *him*? Liss could not understand it. Then she remembered what Quanohtsín, the Sun's Brother, had said, "Those whose souls are heir to our own answer and perform sacrifice." She had no great opinion of the Drip's soul, but still . . . Maybe they wanted to give him advanced lessons in Utter Awfulness. How to bend people the way you want them to go? Maybe if they got him into here and now, they could use him to get at the future? Poor old Apple Lock if Sonny grew up to . . . As she watched, for one crazy, frozen moment, the Seven Kings, in shape and gesture, were an echo of the future. For one moment—some trick of the mind—they recalled the photograph that hung in a gold frame above her grandfather's desk. Seven men. With a newspaper headline below them that read: *Retiring Legislator Lauded by City Notables at Banquet.* Grandfather in the middle, with Councilmen Edward Thomaselli and George "Tiny" Austen, Dr. Motley Washburn, and William Toohey, who was some kind of union official. The ones on the ends were Mr. Malinak, who was president of one of the lodges, and Mr. Cecil, who ran the cemetery and looked like one of his own customers. In Liss's imagination Grandfather-Quanohtsín blurred, and a grown-up Sonny grinned in his place. She blinked, and once more they were seven strangers standing in the morning sun. Sun. . . . Suddenly, she understood something else, too, and had to bite her tongue to keep from crying out to Callie. Moon Maiden, moon Child—the words whirled in her head. Moon. The Sun's rival. Gifts to the Sun. Offerings. How dim she had been! The folk of Abáloc had mingled talk of Cibotlán and sacrifice, and she had understood, but only with the top of her head. The whole idea was so preposterous that it had not really sunk in. They had even joked about it. Now she had visions of some obscure ceremony where these . . . these savages must mean to present her and the Drip to the Sun. It was so unbelievable that she found herself wondering, almost calmly, how they went about it. Did they toss you down the steps or over a cliff between courses at the feast, or what? And why aren't I screaming my head off? The answer was, of course,

that it wasn't likely to do the least bit of good. Except . . .
it might wake Harry up. It seemed to Liss that he looked
positively spellbound at the prospect of all that honor.

Liss found herself hating him. She could half understand
wanting to give the Drip away, but Harry probably wouldn't
lift a finger if they moved to chuck her down the stairs, too.
Why should he? Once she had ratted on him to Miss
Langley when he and Michaelangelo Pucci had a fight on
the playground. After that he made a point of looking
through her as if she weren't there.

Like now. But Callie was watching her uncertainly. Did
she *want* her to screech? Or what? The urgency between
them was almost something you could touch—if your hands
weren't tied. Why didn't Harry say something? He moved
to the head of the broad stair and looked down. The silent
crowd stirred and began to sway, chanting lowly with a
single voice. Except for . . .

Except for the splendid company at the foot of the stair.
They had moved before, slightly, absentmindedly, as a person watching at a window will do. And now they were still,
staring. Liss realized then that those at the front of the
crowd had seen neither Callie nor Harry until Harry moved
forward. The young man in white shook his head, putting
a hand to his brow as if he did not know whether he were
waking or dreaming. There was something familiar about
his face. Brilliant in his gems and feathers, he moved half
a step forward, unsteadily, as if he were drugged or ill.

"Hari! Hari!" he cried.

Harry stared. Liss, startled out of her caution, twisted
free and ran to come up close behind him, with Callie.

"It is I, Lincoas of Abáloc," the young man cried. "Do
not do what they ask! For I am the Chosen One of the
coming feast, and it is a sentence of death."

When Lincoas began to speak, Quanohtsín mastered his
surprise and made a sign. Drums and flutes sounded from

among the seven companies surrounding Lincoas and his companions from Abáloc. The strange music rose as Lincoas shouted, drowning him out at last.

"How do you know my name?" Harry yelled, but the music was a wall between them.

Callie's hands lifted from her pockets and clapped to her mouth. Only Liss saw the movement and the blue-green stone that, caught in the cuff, flew out, bounced wide, and rattled down the long stair.

That was all the children saw. They never saw Lincoas stoop to pick the stone up under cover of the confusion that their disappearance caused.

9

"**B**ut how *did* he know your name?" Callie asked.
"You wanna go back and ask him, you go right ahead, woman," Harry panted, using his hands to sweep earth and leaves over the pile of matted branches they had used to fill up the passage. He had lost his gloves somewhere. Liss wore his hat, flaps down, and Callie's mittens. She jumped up and down, rubbing her arms, sniffling and wheezing from the cold.

"Brrr! I'm j-just lucky I didn't take my boots off and go around in my socks."

"What's your mama going to say when you tell her you've lost your coat?" Callie asked. She managed to squeeze another of the objects they had brought with them out of the chamber into her already bulging pockets.

"Golly, I d-dunno. What'll I *tell* her? She'll make me wear my old one even if the sleeves are too short."

"Oh, sure," Harry drawled. "Your rich granddaddy'll buy you a new one. Two new ones. There. Does that look OK?" He stepped back and looked at the bank of the mound critically.

"Yeah, fine," Callie answered. "Here, stick these into your

pockets. I've run out of room." She handed him the shell cup and a toy animal carved in stone. "And you can give 'em back as soon as we get home, hear? I got a box under my bed I can put them in till we figure what to do with 'em."

He looked at his watch. It read five minutes to four. He shivered. It had all happened so quickly. There were no search parties, no new tracks in the snow, no thaw or fresh snow, no weekday traffic in the town below. It was still Sunday afternoon. But he had entered the passage at, say, a quarter to four, and they had been three days gone. He felt a little the way he always did going up in elevators—as if his stomach had slipped.

"What'll I tell Mother about my coat?" Liss mourned.

"You better think of something quick." Callie pointed. "Somebody's coming."

A tall figure moved through the distant trees, coming from the direction of Liss's house. It stopped.

"Whoever it is isn't gonna climb over the fence," Callie observed.

"Oh, grunch!" Liss's voice squeaked with cold and alarm. "It must be Grandpa."

"We better get out," Harry urged. He pulled at Callie's arm, pausing only to give a warning. "Don't you go talking wild about this to anybody, Liss Mitchell. For all we know, we just passed out in there for a minute. Oxygen starvation. Isn't that what they call it? It makes you queer in the head." He spoke this last slowly, as much to convince himself as her.

Liss, astonished, stopped her jiggling. She opened her mouth to protest, but was silenced by the sharp command called through the trees.

"Melissa? Melissa, you are to come home at once. Who is that you have with you? Melissa? Move!"

"It's Grandpa, all right." She threw the cap to Harry and ran. Callie and Harry plunged down the field and out of sight.

Grandfather was bundled in his black greatcoat, with a green mohair scarf up almost to his nose and a black astrakhan fur hat covering his white hair. Liss wondered why he must always look as if someone had stuck a steel rod down his spine. His thin nose quivered angrily as he spoke.

"Where, if I may ask, is your coat, my dear? And who were those children? Where *is* your coat? Did one of them take it? You can't trust . . . even the children."

Liss was suddenly very warm, her face fiery red. "I threw my coat down a hole." It was true, after a fashion. "You can't trust who?"

Taken aback, her grandfather pursed his lips. His breath frosted out in a cloud. "That sort. Those people who live down in Division Four."

Division Four was the old name of the downtown area south of Center Street, where most of the Negroes lived. But Liss was too afraid of her grandfather to argue. She climbed over the fence and stalked home ahead of him, muttering under her breath, "Why not say it right out, Grandpa? Why don't you say it right out?" She could not find the courage to say it aloud. Tears ran down and made the sniffles worse.

The cold got the better of her, and she ran the last hundred yards, stamping some of the snow from her boots on the back porch and then bursting indoors. Mrs. Calvert, the cook, ordered her back out again.

"Laura waxed this floor only yesterday, and I won't have you dripping all over it!"

"I don't *care*." Liss flung through the swinging door into the hall, past her astonished mother, and up the stairs. On

95

the landing she narrowly missed colliding with Miss Wyre, Sonny's nurse and governess.

Miss Wyre steadied the tea tray she carried and spoke reprovingly.

"Ladies do not galumph, Melissa. And they are more considerate of others. Your poor cousin had a perfectly dreadful nightmare while he was napping. The poor little dear could not bear to tell me about it and didn't even want his hot chocolate and cookies when I brought them. He is finally sleeping restfully. You *must* not wake him."

Liss had forgotten the Drip entirely. At the top of the stairs she sat down to pull off her boots, so that she could go more quietly. In her own room she blew her nose on a wad of tissues and rooted out her furry slippers. Very carefully, she made her way back down the long hallway to the door next to her grandfather's room and eased the knob around. She pushed the door gently, with one finger.

The curtains and blinds were drawn, but Liss could see Sonny lying still and straight, like a stick figure under the covers drawn up over his nose. She tiptoed in. If he weren't so obnoxious, she could almost feel sorry for him. He was supposed to stay indoors all winter—delicate lungs, the Pittsburgh doctor had told Grandpa. Liss had puzzled over his illness. Do lungs "get" delicate? Or do they come that way? The Drip had been right enough until after Uncle Conway and Aunt Gwen were killed in the car accident. Oh, he used to catch a lot of colds and be cranky, but he was bearable. Now, being shut up and having school lessons from simpery Miss Wyre was enough to serve him double-right for all the meanness. Liss softened a little. She turned to tiptoe out again.

"Missy? Is that you?" The reedlike voice quavered. There was always a complaining note to it, not quite a whine.

"I thought you were asleep. I'm sorry."

"I pretended." He pulled the covers down from his face. "Shut the door. I pretended, so old Wirey would go away."

"What's the matter?" She approached cautiously. "You look awful. You're not going to upchuck, are you?"

"I had a nightmare." His flaxen hair was damp, plastered against his pale forehead. "I couldn't tell Wirey. She'd tell Grandfather, and he'd call Doctor Fullsom. Oh, *Missy!*"

To her astonishment, he threw his arms around her and pulled her close. She sat on the edge of the bed and let him cry on her sweater. She stroked the fine hair awkwardly. He was trembling all over.

"What was it?" she asked. "And why would they call the doctor?"

Sonny sniffled. "They always do," he said. He sniffled again, self-pityingly, and announced with a touch of melodrama, "I'm a captive, like in that storybook of yours. *You* know."

Liss quivered with a giggle she managed not to let loose. Sonny *was* something like the boy in *The Secret Garden* had been at the beginning of the story. Only she wouldn't have thought he would care to admit it. Pushing him away, she handed him one of the extra tissues she had stuck in her pocket, not noticing the change in his expression. He had felt her laughter. His mouth tightened a little, and his pale eyes narrowed. She was stupid. He would show her who was smart. And then when she was gone, he would think up something good—something beautiful to serve that black girl right. She had called him names. She hadn't let him do what They wanted. He had had to run. But he would go back, and They would tell him more good things. . . . He blew his nose.

"It was awful," he said slowly, allowing a little catch to sadden his voice. "I was so scared. There was this big operating table, hard as stone, and everything was all fuzzy. And the doctors—there were *lots* of them, funny looking, all with big knives. They were *all* going to operate on me. You won't let Wirey call the doctor, will you?"

"But it was only a dream, silly. Everybody has nightmares sometime." And sometimes, she thought, you weren't sure what was dream and what wasn't. Harry's last words came back to nag at her. That couldn't have been a dream. Three people couldn't all come down with the same dream, could they? She frowned and chewed at her lip, then patted the Drip's shoulder awkwardly.

"Poor kid," she said.

"Ha, ha, ho!" Sonny threw himself back on the pillows. "Made you squirm, you silly worm!"

"O-oo-oh! You nasty little beast!" Furious at having been taken in, Liss slammed out of the room.

Once she was gone, Sonny's look of triumph disappeared. "It *was* just a dream," he whispered. He turned over, pulling the covers tight around his shoulders, and burrowed his head under the pillows. His hand found a worn leather bag, knobby and round with its treasure of marbles, and rubbed it as if it held some magical comfort. "When I'm grown up," he confided to the silk-sheeted mattress, "They promised me, when I'm grown up . . ."

From the hallway, Liss heard her mother and grandfather talking at the foot of the stairs—something about Dr. Washburn, the pastor at St. Dunstan's Church, and about textbooks and a blue sweater. She heard her mother say, "I hope you didn't make it definite, Papa. I'd like to go upstairs and have a word with Melissa first."

"I hardly see that it need concern her."

Liss ran for her own room. Blue sweaters. The girls at St. Dunstan's School wore navy blue sweaters. Grandpa *wouldn't* . . .

Her mother knocked at the door. "May I come in?"

She sat on the bed beside Liss. "Melissa, your grandfather . . ."

"Oh, Mommy, he's *not* going to make me go to St. Dunstan's, is he?"

Mrs. Mitchell raised her eyebrows in surprise. "Well, Missy, if you were listening, perhaps you can tell me what this is all about? Papa stormed in right behind you and didn't even stop to take off his hat before he telephoned Dr. Washburn. Whatever did you do or say? All I could make out was that someone had either stolen your coat or dared you to throw it down a well, and that Fourth Street School was a thoroughly bad influence."

"I was playing with Callie and Harry Rivers," Liss said. "And I did lose my coat down a hole, but it wasn't their idea."

"Callie and Harry Rivers?" Mrs. Mitchell began to understand. "I see. They're in your class, aren't they? And they're black?"

"Yes. Oh, I know what Grandpa says." She mimicked resentfully, " 'Tapps have an obligation to maintain high standards.' And who says what's high? He does. By Grandfather's standards, even *I'm* not good enough to associate with me. Besides," she grumbled, "I'm a Mitchell, not a Tapp."

Her mother's frown disappeared. "Oh, how right you are! And thank goodness, too." She laughed. "When your father was alive, your grandfather used to say, 'I'll never understand Bill Mitchell. He *will* not understand that such things are not *done*.' There are such a lot of good things Papa finds it difficult to understand. There's nothing to do but try to be patient, dear."

"How can I be patient? I don't want to go to St. Dunstan's!"

"You won't have to, then. But what can be so terrible about St. Dunstan's? Or so wonderful about Fourth Street, for that matter? Having afternoons off because of the half-day sessions?"

"No!" Liss reddened. "Well, that was fun at first. But it's mostly because I'd have to be in Mrs. Coffee's class. Before she came up to St. Dunstan's last year, she substituted in our room when Mrs. Agresti had her appendix out. She makes you recite—you know, memorize things, and stand up and reel them off? When you ask her something and she doesn't know the answer, she gets all smiley and says, 'Now let's turn to page ninety-two,' or, 'Now, Melissa, you aren't going to learn it as well if I tell you as if you were to look it up yourself.' "

Mrs. Mitchell looked doubtful. "Yes, but if you *do* learn . . ."

Liss shrugged. "Oh, I suppose we learned what she gave us. But nobody *cared*. Miss Langley, now, she says, 'I don't know,' and makes finding out interesting. And Mrs. Agresti doesn't get all prissy because Tommy Mistovich can figure out the math problems faster than she can. She thinks he's great."

"All right. All right, that's good enough for now." Mrs. Mitchell gave Liss a squeeze. "But *do* be kind to Grandpa. He is right, you know, about what you are losing with the city schools on half-session."

"That's not *our* fault! But I'll try. Really I will." Liss traced the figure on the bedspread with her finger. "But why does he always talk like we're better than other people? I think it only makes everyone unhappy. Him, too."

"Yes. But you see, when he was a senator, he *was* very important, and he did many good things, too. Only, it's all so long ago now, and it hurts him to have lost it." She spoke carefully, trying to be honest and yet make Liss see her love for the old man. "I think that some people who are in their secret hearts unsure of themselves come to think that they can feel secure and important only by seeing other people as somehow weaker or smaller. If people like that are power-ful, it can be a very evil thing . . ."

Like Neolin or Quanohtsín, Liss thought, with a shiver.

". . . and if they haven't any skill or power, they're trapped—unhappy and, well, spiteful."

Liss bit on her thumbnail. "Sonny's like that already. Just since Aunt Gwen and Uncle Conway died." She hesitated. "Oh, Mommy! Why do we have to live *here?*"

Mrs. Mitchell watched her. "We don't *have* to," she said slowly. "I suppose we could find an apartment down in town. It would save me part of the long commute across the river and down to Poole every day. But if Sonny were left here, alone with his Grandpa and Wirey, in all these dark rooms . . ."

"Oh, he'd love it. All that attention, and no me galumph-ing down the hall or picking on him."

"Well . . ." Mrs. Mitchell worried deeply about her brother's child. It almost seemed that Sonny hated them all. At least, the only thing he seemed truly to care for was the one thing he had of his father's: the beautiful old marbles in their worn bag. She could remember her brother Conway playing with them, trying to teach her how to shoot prop-erly. . . . Wild, careless Conway. He had loved his little boy so much. She felt an uncomfortable stirring of con-science. *She* was Sonny's legal guardian. His grandfather was not. In that one thing her brother Conway had defied the old man. What had he wanted her to do? Take him away? Take him away. . . . But there was Melissa to think of, too. She stood up. "Perhaps," she said. "Think about it a while longer, and I will, too. We'll talk about it after Christ-mas if you still want. Agreed? Right now I must go and have a word with Papa." She went out, closing the door after her.

Liss drew her feet up and sat cross-legged on the bed. To be rid of the Drip . . . !

IO

"Well, good morning, Harry!" Miss Langley was surprised. "This is the first time you've beat me in." She put her green bookbag on the desk and went into the cloakroom to hang up her coat. Her voice floated out. "Did Callie set the clock ahead on you?"

"No'm. I just got up early. And it's too cold to fool around outside." He let the U.S. map he had been examining roll back up on its roller.

Sunday's mild thaw had frozen over, and the temperature was down to five below zero. Harry had not slept very well for dreaming of a wild, primeval countryside, of tattooed men, and of long arguments with himself about whether any of it could really have happened, since no time had elapsed at all. Neither of him had won.

Miss Langley came out and sat down to pull her snow boots off. "Were you trying to find something on the map?"

"No. I mean, yeah, but it's not on there."

"Hardly anything is." She made a face at the stubbornness of the second boot. "The scale is too small, and the poor old thing was made in the Year One. Arizona is still the Arizona Territory. But my road atlas is over there on the geography shelf. See if you can find what you want there." She emptied the books and several thick bundles of papers from the green bag. "What we could use is one of those lovely big wall maps that you can draw routes and things on and wipe them off afterwards." She laughed, and her laughter had an edge to it. "But I suppose that when archaeologists come a-digging here in the year 3069, they'll find this same old map in the ruins of Room 206."

Harry looked up, a little confused. "In the ruins?"

She grimaced at the splintered floor and cracked plaster. "This place will have to fall flat before they start thinking of a new school."

"Oh, yeah. Hey, Miss Langley—it isn't in here either."

"What is it you're looking for?"

He hesitated. "Oh, a town. *Quauna* something. Quaunatilcó? Anyhow, I guess there's no such place now. If there ever was."

"It sounds like an Indian name. Almost Mexican. This isn't something for your Social Studies report, is it?"

"No." He was startled. "Oh man, I forgot all about that. When's it for?"

"Don't worry. I'm going to have to postpone some of the reports anyway." She was thoughtful for a moment and rubbed her eyes as if they ached, but soon brightened and said, "Is this Quaunatilcó of yours an old Indian settlement? You might take a look at the Geological Survey maps over at Seese Library. Those maps have everything on them: villages, farmhouses, even the old Indian fortifications. And you might look for place names that sound similar. It's surprising how place names have a way of sticking."

Harry closed the atlas carefully, as if it were breakable. His mind raced. Apple Lock—Abáloc. That wasn't the kind of thing you invented in a dream. What were the rivers they had crossed? He couldn't remember. His heart thumped. But then habit took hold again. So what? What if it were all true? Who would believe it? What did it have to do with the price of chewing gum, or anything else, for that matter? It wasn't worth getting heated up over or coming out sounding like an idiot.

Misunderstanding his thoughtful look, Miss Langley went on. "It might *be* a good idea for a report, you know? Local place names reflecting local history?"

Harry shrugged. "Maybe. I dunno." He ambled to his seat.

"Perhaps not," she agreed solemnly, unwilling to let him

slip back into his usual silence. "It would mean a lot of research—more time than you would want to spend."

"You putting me down, Miss Langley?" He assumed a look of wounded reproach.

"No, putting you *on*." She laughed. "Come on, Harry. Couldn't you at least do Apple Lock and the Edge and, say, Simmer Flats?"

"Maybe." He got his books out for English and math and science. He already knew what Apple Lock meant, but she wouldn't believe it. Why should she?

Anne Palisser and Jack Penrod came in, and several others not far behind them. Miss Langley began to take the roll, to save time during the homeroom period for her announcement.

"No school at *all* after Thanksgiving?" Ralph Hagedorn's voice was loudest, riding over the buzz and the muffled cheers that came from several seats at the back.

"Why not, Miss Langley?" Liss almost wailed. She saw St. Dunstan's lurking outside the door of 206.

Miss Langley explained. "Superintendent Moon, and all the rest of us, had hoped that, among other things, we could save enough money to finish the semester by closing the Grove Avenue School and bussing the Grove children over here for the afternoon session." In a drier tone she added, "But a number of parents seem more upset that the Junior Basketball Tournament and the Christmas play had to be cut out than that Grove Avenue had to be closed. The City Council has agreed to a special election in January to try again to get the new school bond issue and the raise in school tax passed, but that isn't much help right now. We have barely enough money left in this semester's funds for keeping the teachers, the busses, and the furnaces going for four weeks. Mr. Moon decided it would be best to save it for January."

"It's all so *dumb*," Charlie Baker complained. "My pop says S and S is doing better right now than almost any mill on the river. Nobody's laid off, and everybody's taking home *pots* of overtime pay. But you'd think it was the original Poorsville."

"Maybe *you've* got pots," someone muttered behind the cover of a desk top.

Mary Lou Washington raised her hand. "Miss Langley? You mean you won't get paid for December? What'll you do for Christmas?"

"Thanks for the good thought, Mary Lou." Miss Langley smiled. "But I'll be going home to Poole for a Christmas with two dozen relatives, two turkeys, and a roast goose. I'll manage."

The bell rang. Miss Langley nodded. "I'll see you all fourth period." The little D'Agostino girl paused by her desk on the way out to whisper, "You'll come back after Christmas, won't you, please?"

Miss Langley smiled briefly. "Of course." Then she grinned. "Unless somebody offers me a nice cushy job in a coal mine." She shooed Teeny along and went to the blackboard to write out the assignment for her first period class. Thank heavens it would be a short week. On most Mondays the week stretched out ahead of her like an endless corridor lined with classrooms. Since Fourth Street School had been on emergency double session, she taught eight classes a day, except Tuesdays, which was assembly day. One class was a girls' gym class ("Next thing to a free period," the principal had apologized) as there was no longer a special gym teacher. She watched her hand automatically writing, *"All books are to be turned in at the end of class on Wednesday."* Funny, she thought. Only Jack Penrod and Wally Gowins and Doris Austin had cheered, and Jack had shut up when Ralph gave him a punch in the back. *"I love 206,"* she wrote on the board, with curlicues around it. Underneath, in a flowing longhand, she added,

But I hate school.
True or false?
Choose one.
Put the other one in a paper bag.

The first period students poured in, and she erased it hurriedly and went on with the assignment.

After fourth period, Liss and Callie stayed behind to ask whether they could change the topics for their local history reports. At Sunday supper Liss and her grandfather had been very polite to each other, and when the conversation touched on the report, he had suggested that an understanding of the records kept by the County Records Office was basic to any such historical research. When he mentioned that it was possible to trace the history of houses and property as well as people, she had immediately thought of the Edge. Who *did* it belong to? She had decided that, dull as it sounded, she would like to report on the County Records Office. Callie's question was more vague. Did anybody know who had lived in the valley before the first settlers?

"The Senecas? I think it may have been the Senecas, Callie, but there may have been Shawnees and Delawares, too."

"No ma'am. Before them, even." She took a deep breath. "Like who built that big mound down at Moundsville?"

Miss Langley looked a little surprised and very much interested. "I don't really know, and I'm not sure anyone else does either. You've picked a real mystery. Do you know that there are thousands of mounds? They're down along the Ohio Valley, and the Mississippi, and even up into Wisconsin. My—a friend of mine who teaches archaeology at Poole College told me that. I grew up around here and never knew it. Most people don't. Let's see . . . you might check whether Seese Library has any books that can tell you something. Ask Mrs. Buttery at the reference desk. And the encyclopedia *might* have something."

On their way out Liss whispered, "She was going to say 'my boy friend,' I bet. I bet my mother knows who he is. She works at the college."

"Ask her who teaches ark-whatever-it-is," Callie said. They were on the front stairs before she spoke what was really on her mind. "I don't care how Harry tries to wiggle out of it. We really *were* in Abáloc. How can you and Harry talk about puzzles and a lot of dusty old courthouse records when there are all those people in trouble?" She was a bit embarrassed at how smugly virtuous that sounded. It wasn't the whole truth, either. It wasn't as much the people as the clean, bright unspoiled world they lived in. She ached to think of the forest that had once stood where they walked now. To be there, and alone . . .

Liss stopped on the bottom step. "You mean, go back?" She was alarmed. "Even if we *could* get back, we couldn't help. It was us in trouble, too. We'd just be in the frying pan with all the rest of them."

Callie pushed at the bar, opening the door. "You don't know that. Maybe we'd land the same place as before, right there where the mound is."

She did not say what was uppermost in her mind: that it would be a lot better to find some way back on their own hook than to have the snowmen come shlumphing around Apple Lock, looking to drag them back. Or worse, to have them stay and get realer and realer every day, like the Ugly-Wugglies in *The Enchanted Castle*, the book Mama gave her last month for her twelfth birthday ("Not 'realer and realer'—more and more real!" she imagined her mother correcting). Or they might start taking people over, like those giant slugs in one of Harry's science-fiction books. She shuddered, and not from the cold.

"And do what?" Liss insisted.

Harry was waiting for them at the corner, stamping his feet and breathing into his mittens. "Lookit who's wearing her dress-up coat! Hey, what are you two glooming for? You coming home for lunch, Cal?" He was angry when he heard that Callie wanted to go back up to the Edge again. He forgot his pose of scientific disbelief, betraying himself by agreeing with Liss. "What *could* we do to unpickle their pickle?"

Callie rounded on him. "See! You *do* know we didn't have some nutty kind of three-way dream!"

"All right, all right." He danced along and back on the ice. "But don't you get it? It's all over already. They're done and gone. Phht-t. It was all some kind of weird accident. They don't have anything to do with us. Besides," he said, "we couldn't get back again if we wanted to."

"How do you know?" Liss asked.

"It figures," he said vaguely. "Come on, Cal. Unless you're gonna skip lunch. It's too cold to stand here and flap." He fled off and away up Fourth Street toward South Hill Road.

After lunch Harry got dressed to go out again. "Don't forget the ashes," his mother reminded. She was pleasantly surprised when he didn't try to put it off, for his mind seemed miles away. He carried the two full ash buckets up the outside cellar steps and carefully scattered the ashes down the icy driveway so that his father could get the car up when he came home. He was on the day turn this week.

When the driveway was finished, Harry headed downtown, looking for Eddie Williams and Mel Brown. He went all the way down Center Street, past the Fairlawn Hotel, the hole-in-the-wall taxicab office, the Tavern, Sam's newsstand, and the Serbian-American Club. Except for the block that had the County Courthouse, Seese Library, the American Legion, and Weebles', practically every other building was a bar. The only difference among them was that some were dirtier than others. Mel and Eddie weren't at Smitty's Diner or the music store or the Elite Drugstore, where the men played pool in the back room, so Harry gave up and headed across Front Street to Simmer Flats and the river.

It was too cold to sit on the abandoned loading dock and look for interesting junk in the water, so he walked along the crumbling, overgrown brick-paved esplanade for a way, watching the dirty river and swirls of detergent suds slide past. Closing his eyes, he could see the sycamores and sassafras, and the blue-and-silver water like a broad ribbon between the green hills. "Does it *got* to be like this?" He yelled to the empty flats. A stray dog froze in alarm and then hurried away. Harry jammed his hands deep in his coat pockets and kicked a brick into the river.

His little notebook. Through the lining, Harry felt it at the bottom of his inside pocket. He tore off a mitten to reach in and pull it out, and flipped the pages wildly, his fingers shaking with the cold and with excitement.

"Oh, man." He whispered it.

The strange signs leaped out from the page, and below them sprawled the even stranger words: A PLEVROW OR REGOOWAYS O ABALOCK.

He said them aloud, and they shimmered in the crackling air.

All the hurrying way home, he kept telling himself that it was just "interesting." There wasn't a hope of translating hieroglyphs. He knew that. Not without something like the Rosetta Stone, where the same thing was written out in some language people still knew. Up in his own room he took the bedside lamp into his closet, where Callie wouldn't interrupt him. His mother said she had gone to the library, but he didn't mean to take a chance. There were too many things to think out, knots to unravel. He propped the little notebook against the door and sat cross-legged, staring at it with his chin in his hands.

Tuesday, on the way out of math class, Harry slipped a folded piece of paper to Michaelangelo Pucci and sauntered on ahead. On it he had written:

ꓘᴇᴇᴌꓨ/ꖎᴆꖌ ꓨᴇᴌ ᴌ⅃ᴆꖌ ᴌᴦᴊᴌꖌ
ꓩꓨ ᴆᴆᴆ ᴌᴇᴐᴆ/ᴉᴆᴆ ꓨᴇᴌ ᴦᴆ
ꖌꓨᴆ ᴌᴌᴌᴆꓨ ᴌꓨ ꖌꓨᴆ ꓨᴌᴊ/ꓨᴊᴦᴦ

All of which spelled out, in the old box-and-dot cipher Pooch had shown the class, "POOCH—BET YOU CAN'T CRACK MY NEW CODE—SEE YOU IN THE ALLEY BY THE PUB—HARI." Harry liked spelling his name that way. It had an elegant, somehow African, look to it.

Pooch caught up to him outside of 206. "You're on. See you later."

They went in the side door of Pucci's Grocery and up the stairs to the second floor. Pooch opened the door into the front room, a large unused storeroom.

"My office!" He waved his hand grandly.

The whole of one side of the room was neatly stacked with crates, old-fashioned display cases, planks, carpenters' horses, a bundle of old window shades, and a stepladder. Two doors leaned against the wall. Across the broad cleared space, there were two chairs and a battered rolltop desk. The end wall, beside the hall door, was lined with stock shelves.

"My pop moved all this stuff in here when they put in the frozen food cases and the new cold storage downstairs. It's been here ever since." He selected a book from the shelf, opened the desk, and pulled up a chair. "This isn't a 'code,' you know. Come on, where'd you get it?" He unfolded the sheet Harry had copied the letter-signs from Abáloc onto and began searching through the book to see if he could find anything like them.

"Never mind that." It was a question Harry had decided to evade. "I thought it was hieroglyphs, you know. But then I figured if it was, there wouldn't be so many shapes so near alike. I mean, they'd be more like picture writing, wouldn't they? So, couldn't this be an alphabet?"

"You mean a cipher?"

"Well, yeah, I guess so." He supposed that a strange alphabet might in a sense be a cipher of the familiar Roman alphabet, but he wasn't sure.

"The figures in a cipher lots of times are near alike. But if it's a cipher, it's not like any in my book. And it's hard to break ciphers. You got to have some kind of foothold. The book can tell us how to start, but that's all. Here: these are the letters that turn up oftenest." Pooch took a sharpened pencil stub from one of the desk drawers and jotted down the letters E T A O N R I S H D. "Then we make a list of these weird alphabet signs," he explained, "and count how often each of 'em turns up. If we're lucky, that'll give us E at least." He copied the strange figures in a column down the sheet. "And if there are any doubles, that helps. In English we got lots of double E's and S's or T's. See?"

"Um." Harry had a sinking feeling. "What if—well, what if it isn't English? Does that mean you wouldn't know what sounds you get most of?" He knew the answer before he finished the sentence.

Pooch chewed at the end of the pencil. He watched Harry's face. "It'd be impossible. Even if we guessed right at the E's and T's and such, you'd only have those letters. From there on a lot of it's guessing, trying this and that. You're stuck if you don't know the language. You haven't got a handle to get hold of it with." He frowned. "Why? Why do you think it isn't English?"

Harry looked glum. "Just a hunch," he lied.

Pooch could find nothing in the book to help with such a problem. The two boys sat frowning in concentration for a while, but got nowhere. It was as bad, Harry thought, as trying to solve a crossword puzzle written in Martian. Impossible.

"Well, let's try for the E's, anyhow." Pooch counted up the signs and found that ⊖ appeared most often, ten times in all. "OK, say that makes it the E sound." **L** appeared eight times, and ○ five times. Reading them as T and A, he wrote under the signs:

⊖·⌐⊗○⊙⊓**L**·⊞○⌐⊖·△⊖⌐⊖⊞
  E   A   T   A E   E E

⊖·⊙⊚⌐⊞⊗⊟○△**L**⊟·**L**⊓·⌐⊙⌐⊖⊖·⌐⊗⊖⊟⊓**L**⊟⊖⊟
E   A T   T   E   E   E T E

L⊓·⊓⊚⊙**L**⊟⊖⊟·**L**·○⊖○⊗**L**⊙
 T   T E   T A A T

"It looks like a bunch of junk to me. It might not be an alphabet cipher at all," Pooch said. But he did not intend giving up. "Here, we oughta keep these guesses separate, not run 'em all together. This paper isn't big enough. I'll go downstairs and get us a piece of butcher paper. Here, you stare at this." He handed the sheet to Harry. "Sometimes if you stare hard enough, a word'll jump up and hit you right between the eyes."

Harry waited until the door closed and then took out his notebook. There looked to be no way that A PLEV-ROW OR REGOOWAYS O ABALOCK could fit into the sprinkling of letters that E, T, and A gave. Where there were double O's in the one, there were no doubles in the other. He glared at the paper, as if by looking he could will everything to fall into place. He stared until his eyes unfocused and the figures became a shimmer edged with purple and a white brighter than the paper: patterns, not letters . . .

And then he saw it. One tiny pattern repeated in the signs and the letters. The same sound first and third.

Abalock.

Abaloc. A-blank-A-blank-blank-blank.

He danced all the way to the window and back.

"My sister copied it down in a hurry," Harry said, in apology for the uneven printing. "It's the old name for Apple Lock, see? Even before the French and Indian War Indians." His caution disappeared in the rush of excitement. "What do you think, man? Look, it would make **L** mean O instead of T, and ⊕ has to be either C or K, since the word's a letter too short to have both."

Pooch spread the butcher paper out on the floor and knelt down eagerly. "C, I think. Because it's so much like A and B. What do you bet? And that double squiggle would be the L sound. That makes . . ." He recopied the strange signs, and beneath them filled in the letters they had so far:

⊖·Γଃ♦ৎ□L·Ⅲ♦꠸⊖·△⊖꠸⊖Ⅲ
  E   LA O AE   EE

⊖·☯ᇓⅢⴲ⊖⊟♦△L⊟·L□·Γ⊖꠸⊓⊖⊖·Γଃ⊖⊟□L⊟⊖⊟
E   AO O E   E LE   OE

L□·□ᇓ꠸L⊟⊖⊟·L·♦⊖♦ଃL⊕
 O   O E O ABALOC

"Now, there's a load of nothing," Harry muttered after he had pulled the sheet around to have a look. Puzzle as he might, he could see no shape to it. "And these other words won't fit in front of 'Abáloc.' One's too short and the other's too long. Unless . . . unless there's other ways of spelling them? In our alphabet, I mean?"

Pooch grinned. "You knocking your sister's spelling?"

Harry straightened slightly. "No, man. And don't you, either. I only meant, you could spell *fish* as *p-h-i-s-c-h,* and it would come out sounding the same."

Pooch nodded, writing as he talked. "*Regooways.* If it was the word before *Abáloc,* it would have to be R-I-G-O-blank-E-S, then, because of this O and E." He chewed on the pencil, then said, "It has to be an I after the R, since we've already got E. What about trying U in the blank? If you put in a W, it would be a GO or GOW sound—in English, anyhow—instead of GOO."

Rigoues, if they were right, gave them five new letters: R, I, G, U, and S. With these, the full inscription was expanded to read:

⊙·ΓꙄꙨꙨꙨⴑⳐ·ꙥꙨꙆꙨ·△ꙨꙆⴺⴱ
E LAGRO A E   E E

⊙·ꙨꙆⴺⴲꙨꙨꙨꙨ△⊔Ꙡ·ⴺꙠ·ΓꙨꙆꙟꙨꙨ·ΓꙨꙨꙨⴺꙠꙨꙨ
E I   ISA OS OR E UE   LE ROUES

ⴺꙠ·ꙨꙨꙨꙆꙠꙨꙨ·ⴺ·ꙨꙨꙨꙨⴺꙨ
OR RIGOUES O ABALOC

"There's our O-R," Harry exclaimed. "If it's that close, we *got* to be on the right track. Blank-L-E-blank-R-O-U-E-S. . . . There's a Blank-L-E-blank-R-O for you." He leaned back in the chair and for a long time scowled at the blanks. "Hey, try PLEVROUES instead of PLEV-ROW. That might be 'books' instead of 'book.'"

This gave "E PLAGRO ＿A＿E ＿E＿E＿ E ＿I＿＿ ISA＿OS OR PE＿ ＿UE PLEVROUES OR RIGOUES O ABALOC." And there they stuck fast.

"You got no more words, we get no more sounds, no more letters." Pooch shrugged unhappily. "Where'd you and Callie get these words, anyhow? Why the heck didn't you find out what the whole thing said?"

"It's a lo-o-ong story," Harry said, trying halfheartedly to turn it into a joke. "The lady who had the book couldn't read it either." He wondered, though, whether she might not be able to recognize the words that belonged to some of these bits and pieces of sounds they had. He pushed the thought away. That would mean going back, and he wasn't about to chance meeting the Seven Kings again—the walking Persian carpets, as Liss called them.

"Angelo?" Mrs. Pucci called from the third floor landing. "Angelo, your papa's coming up for his lunch this minute. Hurry and wash your hands, please. We're late as it is."

"I gotta go." Pooch brushed the dust from his trousers. "You know, there's something funny about that alphabet. Do you have to go right home for lunch? I'll be back down as quick as I can."

Harry waited restlessly. He couldn't just *tell* Pooch. You couldn't tell a guy something like that and expect him to believe it. You'd have to . . . He jumped, startled by a knock at the door.

"Hi, Rivers. Pucci around?" Ralph Hagedorn stuck his head in at the door.

"Upstairs. Eating lunch." Harry stooped and rolled up the butcher paper.

"I'll wait, I guess." Ralph pulled off his cap and gloves and brought a waxed-paper-wrapped hamburger out of each pocket. "What's that thing? You guys still fooling around with codes?"

"No, this is something else." Harry's stomach rumbled at the ground beef and onion smell. "Hey, you want to sell me that other burger? We could go over to Smitty's for more after Pooch comes down."

"OK. Twenty cents."

Harry munched thoughtfully. Through a mouthful, he asked, "You know that report you gave in science? On space travel in the future? You say those spacemen will go so fast and far that, when they land, we've gotten older faster than they have?"

"Un-huh. Why?"

"Well—is there any way it could work the other way around?"

Ralph swallowed. "You mean, so they'd get back before they'd *left?*"

"Yeah. I guess. It sounds kind of dumb when you put it that way."

Ralph swung his chair around and straddled it, arms resting on the back. "Let's see," he said, half seriously. "Instead of speeding up and going far out, you'd have to slow *down,* slower than dead stop." He laughed at Harry's skeptical look. "Well, 'dead stop' is really still moving, isn't it, when the whole earth is still going around? Maybe that's what a time machine would have to be: something that could go slower than dead stop. But you could only go backwards, then." He grinned.

Harry thrust his hands deep in his pockets and walked casually toward the front window, to look down at the dingy bars and shops along Center Street. "Going back in time's impossible? I mean, does anybody think it *is* possible?"

"Our next-door neighbor does," Ralph quipped. He was startled to see Harry turn so quickly. "Old Mrs. Knopsnyder," he explained. "She's a real nut. She gives séances and 'communes with the spirits.' "

Harry was impatient. "I don't mean that kind of junk, man. I mean, look: if a guy said to you he had been, say, upstairs here in Pucci's Grocery. OK? Then, *zap*, he found himself up a big old tree near the center of a village that used to be here maybe a thousand years ago. . . . OK, OK!" Harry could hardly stand Ralph's grin. He had to force himself to go on. "Anyhow, suppose he says suddenly *zap!* He's right back here? Come on, Raf! Knock it off, man. Look at it like it was a math problem: A minus B and all. Now. How would he get back to the same spot in the past again?"

"Like a math problem?" Ralph drew a long, solemn face. "Well, my son," he said. And then he cracked up. "You'll have to ask Mistovich that one. He's the math genius. Whoever this guy of yours is, he's got some problem. With his *brain*. Some wack! My old man would say, 'If he wanted to go back, he should take a hair of the dog that bit him.' "

Harry's chagrin would have boiled over into anger if Pooch hadn't come in just then, bringing two oranges, half a loaf of bread, a knife, and the end of a salami.

"Ho, Raf. Here, you two. Have some. The salami's homemade." He unloaded the food onto the desk. "Papa says, 'If you can't sit still, Angelo, take the rest of your lunch outa the room and leave me to enjoy my soup and my headache in peace.' " He lifted a crate from one of the stacks and sat on it.

Harry unrolled the paper, and they explained the puzzle to Ralph. Ralph contemplated the inscription from all angles, turning the paper thoughtfully. When he looked up, his eyes were crossed. "Have you consulted a doctor?" he asked in a deep and solemn voice.

Harry laughed and hit him a glancing blow on the shoulder. "Come on off it, you clown. This is serious."

Convinced only after much argument that it *was* serious, Ralph settled down to trying some of the many possible letter combinations in the remaining blanks. After half an hour the boys decided that approach was useless.

"I dunno. There's something weird about this alphabet," Pooch muttered. He kicked at the desk in frustration.

After an hour—in which Ralph turned to leafing through a pile of old *National Geographics*—Pooch sat up and announced in an astonished voice, "Man, I *knew* something was bugging me!" He grabbed the large sheet of paper and went on excitedly. "You remember I said it looked like a cipher? Well if it isn't, it sure as heck must have something to do with our alphabet." Pooch wrote out the alphabet, numbering the letters, and put the known signs under the proper letters.

"You can get along without J and Y and use I instead. Maybe that's what we got here. Look."

"The shapes. Is that what you mean?" Ralph spoke around his final salami sandwich.

"Yes. The ones we know in the first five are based on a circle; then the next bunch are curlicues; then two angle shapes; and we know four of this last five are squares. In an alphabet you'd expect every shape to be more different, like the sounds are different. These aren't. And it hasn't got anything to do with vowels or kinds of consonants either."

"No. It's the order, isn't it?" Harry frowned. One puzzle only led to another. If this strange alphabet *was* somehow related to the Roman alphabet, what then? Wheels within wheels. He squinted. After a while something struck him— something so beautifully simple that surely it must be wrong. "Look here, Pooch. Suppose the change in the pattern is the same in the other signs as it is in the first bunch?

"Um. I think that's it. Circle, line across, line down, *blank*, line right. D could be line left." He drew a $\ominus$ under

D. "Skip F for now. Three squiggles with two gaps . . . um. No, you'd have to reverse it: right, left, then down, up and double."

This gave:

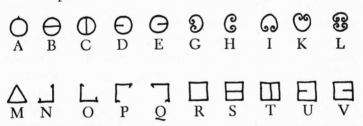

Harry pointed out the ℗ in the inscription itself, and they knew they must be on the right track. Three more undeciphered signs from the inscription— ⌐⌐, ⌐, and ▯ — fitted neatly into patterns. Their excitement grew.

"What's left?" Ralph asked. "There are still seven letters without signs."

"Only the triangle's left. But we don't really need . . ."

"Look," Harry interrupted. "This space in front of these angle things. There are only four of them and five of everything else. What do you bet they're broken triangles?"

"And the triangle is M! That's all we need," Pooch crowed. "See, you can use V for F and U for W. There's no X and no Z, but it doesn't really matter, you guys! We got it!"

The alphabet as it stood contained twenty letters:

○	⊖	⊕	⊖	⊖	⊗	⊖	⊙	℗	⊛
A	B	C	D	E	G	H	I	K	L

△	⌐	⌐	⌐	⌐	□	⊟	⊞	⊟	⊟
M	N	O	P	Q	R	S	T	U	V

Pooch filled in the blanks at the top of the large sheet, and the three of them crowded together to read it.
E PLAGRO TANE MENET E KINTISAMOS OR PENQUE PLEVROUES OR RIGOUES O ABALOC.

Harry and Pooch pummeled each other. Harry rolled on the floor.

"Great," said Ralph. "You guys are great. Very impressive job. Clever. Brilliant, even. But what the ding-dong does it mean? 'My grandmother's cat wears garters'?"

Harry sat up lugubriously, a streak of dust across his forehead. "It might as well," he said. Now that he had it, he was really stuck, really caught. Abáloc needed it; he had it. They would know if the whole of it made sense. And once they knew the sounds, they could puzzle out the *Book of the Kings*. Slowly, reluctantly, he began the story at the beginning.

Harry kicked himself all the way home. Melonhead Rivers! Of course they hadn't believed it. Why should they? Still, they hadn't absolutely *dis*believed it, even with the Abáloc alphabet suspiciously related to their own. They wanted to see the cup and bowl and other treasures from the mound. Harry knew Ralph half suspected the alphabet was a put-up job. Pooch didn't, though. Maybe, Harry figured, somebody actually did make it up from the Roman alphabet and give it to Abáloc longer ago than they could remember. No, that couldn't be. Old bleeding heart Rivers, he thought, kicking at a chunk of ice. He could just see what he would end up doing—chasing ahead of a flock of Persian carpets, looking for Abáloc and yelling, "Come and get your alphabet!" Maybe he couldn't play it so cool any more, but if he had to stick his neck out, he wished it could be for something that sounded more heroic and less dingaling. Why couldn't they figure it out for themselves? He supposed that Erilla thought the signs were, well, magic —not sounds. That ancestor (Neolin's?) who talked them into chucking the books in the first place was some old snake. The less they knew, the more power *he* had, and he could teach whoever was to come after him. Keep It All in the Family. But Neolin was the biggest ratfink of all. Three guesses what he had in his head, and the first two don't count. Old Greasy-Locks thought if he delivered Abáloc up to Cibotlán, he'd get to be King Number Eight. King Neolin of Abáloc-in-Cibotlán.

Out of breath, Harry stopped at the top of Third Street, where it ran into South Hill Road. The streets and snowy roofs were already a pale gray with soot and grime. Only the hilltops were clean. He gave a whoop and skated along the street. A hair of the dog? There just *might* be a way to get back and not get bit.

At home, up in his room, he took his father's old field glasses and propped his elbows on the windowsill to examine the ridge and the Edge. Afternoon sunshine lit them

brightly against the sullen eastern sky. Within the wood, he imagined he could distinguish the dark shape against trees and snow that was the mound. Focusing more carefully, he was sure. It was like a shadow, a long silhouette slightly bulkier at both ends and more so at the middle. You could see that from here more clearly than up close. It was the southern end he needed to know about: whether that other burial chamber was still there.

12

"What's *he* doing here?" Harry jerked his head toward Jack Penrod, who followed along the alley, keeping well behind them.

Eddie Williams and Ralph turned to look.

"Old Square just knows something's up," Eddie said. "Come on, man. My ears are froze."

"Whatta you bet Penrod gets his nose froze?" Ralph cracked. "You can see it twitchin' and snifflin' clear from here. Like an ugly old hound dog."

"He must've heard Pooch this morning," Eddie said, "telling Mel and me about his pop letting you guys use the storeroom."

Harry grinned. "Maybe he thinks it's some little-kid thing, like a secret club, and he wants in. Wait till he sees the girls are in on it. Some of 'em are helping my sis bring the stuff down."

"Hey, let's tell him for initiation he's gotta be Prince Charming for a day to one of the girls!" Ralph kissed an imaginary hand. "Like Marie, maybe. She's always making eyes at somebody."

Eddie got the hiccups from laughing.

"Come on," Harry said. "Nobody's *that* bad, not even Penrod."

They trooped through Pucci's side door, stamping the snow from their feet, and up the stairs. Pooch had already started work in the storeroom. There were nails to hang their coats on, and crates along the wall from the desk to the front window.

"For a bench, see? Come on, let's move some of this stuff out into the hall so we can get at the display cases." Pooch wrestled one of the doors over onto its side edge. "Pop's got a couple of those old-fashioned biscuit bins with glass tops, too. He says 'better a museum case than a dust-catcher.' "

Jack Penrod appeared, to lounge in the doorway. "Museum! Is that what you dum-dums are doing?" He sneered. "I was once at a museum. Museum: that's a big building *full* of dust-catchers."

"We didn't *think* you'd be interested," Ralph said witheringly.

"Why not? I bet I got more stuff a museum would want than you and your black buddies put together. A *real* museum."

"Lotsa dust-catchers, huh?" Harry said. "Come on, Penrod, move it. We want to get these doors out." He shoved past, bumping Jack against the doorframe.

"OK, OK." Jack grumbled. He flattened against the wall and watched them down the hallway and up the stairs. He waited until they were at the top, starting up the attic steps. "Now, if I was you," he called, "I'd take those carpenters' horses and those doors and make me a couple of worktables."

"Which one of us goes down and busts him in the head?" Eddie drawled.

Callie, Liss, Mary Lou Washington, and Marie Kuparik arrived to find the cases in a neat row along one wall, a makeshift but sturdy table by the wide front windows, and another in the middle of the room. Of the original clutter only a small pile remained, in one corner. The girls emptied their pockets of the mound treasure Callie had kept hidden since Sunday, and everyone crowded around, full of questions, to handle and examine each object. The girls tried on the string of pearls and viewed themselves in the strange, shimmery mirror. The bowl and cup and medallion went from hand to hand. Finally, they were arranged in one of the old glass cases on a shelf hastily dusted with a tissue.

"They look kind of lonely," Marie said. She had been included because she sat in class between Liss and Mary Lou and had to pass the message to meet at the Rivers house after lunch. "Couldn't we paint the shelves? My father has some almost-empty cans of paint in the cellar, but it would be enough, I think. I could ask if we could have them."

"There was something else." Callie frowned, not listening. She didn't care about the stupid cases. The stuff had belonged to *people*. Lost people. Lost. . . . She went to where her coat hung and felt in the pockets. "I didn't remember it before. There was a stone—a pretty blue-green stone."

Liss looked up. "You dropped it. Yes, you did. And I think it must've bounced all the way down those stairs." She signaled with her eyebrows. "You know, *those* stairs. I thought you knew it was gone."

Callie and Harry exchanged startled glances and then pointedly avoided looking at each other. Harry, Pooch, Eddie, and Ralph went to confer in one corner, while the girls made a list of things needed: *Paint. Brushes. Newspapers t. cover flr. Shirt cardboards for ~~sines~~ signs.* Callie sat on a crate, absentmindedly doodling flowers on a scrap of paper and begrudging everyone their enthusiasm and busyness. It had all been so . . . so special, and then Liss and Harry had to go dragging in everybody and his bucket and spoil it all. Didn't he see how Abáloc was so much more important than Apple Lock? Worse off, anyhow. So far. She bit at her lip and began absentmindedly twisting her short hair into little spikes.

Jack Penrod spoke loudly. "I don't suppose anybody here has any real Indian axes or arrowheads or grinding stones. If you all weren't so stuck up, I'd let you put mine in some of that empty space you got."

"Where they from?" Pooch asked. "The Five-and-Dime?"

"Aw, come on, you guys! They're for real. They're not even made-on-the-reservation-for-tourists kind of real. They're *real* real. My great-grandfather found 'em when he was a kid, in some old caves downriver where the Indians used to camp."

Ralph nudged Harry and then addressed everyone. "Why not? Why don't we make it anything that's old and from around here? My dad's got some neat fossils from when they cut into the ridge to widen the highway. I know he'd let us have them for a while. They're heavy, though, some of them. I'll need some help to bring them down."

Jack already had his coat on. "I'll go get my stuff, too," he said.

The others got their coats, and as Jack left, Harry surreptitiously slipped a wad of folded papers out of the desk and into his pocket. He nodded to Eddie and Pooch, and they followed Ralph out the door.

Harry stuck his head back in. "We'll be a while. Somebody oughta be thinking up a zingy name for this place."

"And we could make a sign for the door," Mary Lou said. She wrote *Door sign* below *Broom* and *D. rags.*

"Knock, knock. Anybody home?"

Liss opened the door a crack. "What are *you* doing here? It's Sandy and Erna," she said over her shoulder. "What do you want?"

"To come in." Sandy McGonigle grinned. "We were over at Smitty's, and we saw you come down the hill. What's up? Are any of the boys here?"

"No." Liss answered cautiously, opening the door a bit wider. "Why?"

Sandy squeezed past her and looked around. "Because Teeny's downstairs. She didn't want to come up if they were here."

"I'll just get her." Erna handed Liss the large bundle she was carrying, and then went to the banister, hung over, and called. "Teeny, honey, you can come on up. That was all of them we saw goin' out."

Teeny D'Agostino was almost as small as a second- or third-grader. She was pale, dark-haired, and very pretty, but painfully shy. "I'm sorry," she said, flushing. "But they're so big and loud, they always scare me. And when they call me funny names, I don't know what to do."

" 'Teeny Weeny Scallopini'?" Liss was surprised. She took Teeny's coat while Sandy sat on the floor to pull off Teeny's boots and snowpants. "But that's because they *like* you!"

"It's almost *mushy* compared to what they call me." Sandy grinned. She was a big-boned, cheerful girl with reddish blond braids. "Yoicks! Why does your mother have to wrap you up in ten layers as if you were an onion? No wonder you're always last outa school. Mmph . . . there!" She stood up and looked around, putting her hands on her hips.

"Now. What's all the mystery?"

Erna and Sandy broke into giggles at each new turn in Liss's story. Mary Lou and Marie showed both fascination and disbelief and asked a dozen questions. While a defensive Liss was saying, "I don't care if you believe it. It's all the same to me," Teeny went to the glass case and opened the sliding door. She touched the medallion and turned the iridescent cup in her hands.

"I believe it," she said wonderingly. She turned, her eyes shining with excitement. "But what . . . why, where's Callie gone?"

"Gone?" Liss was startled. "Oh, great pumpkins!" Her surprise became alarm. "It was that blue stone. That's what set her to moping. Oh, she *daren't* go back for it! She'll never get back out. We got to stop her." Her very real panic alarmed the others, and as she grabbed for her coat, they were only a moment in doing the same.

"Wait for me," Teeny wailed. She reached for the old-fashioned snow leggings her mother insisted she wear over her skirt and tights.

"Oh, for Pete's sake," Sandy yelled. "Just get your boots on and come." She hurried back to help and then virtually yanked Teeny out of the room and down the stairs. They were buttoning their coats awkwardly as they raced up Third Street. Erna panted alongside, slowed down by her bundle.

"This sure is gonna be the fastest uphill-shoeleather-laundry-delivery I ever made," she gasped. "It's a good thing I gotta go this way anyhow."

Callie had a long head start, and Liss did not catch up until she was dragging loose the last of the matted branches hiding the passage to the mound chamber.

"Where do you think you're going?" Liss's breath came raggedly.

"Crazy," Callie snapped. "You coming along?"

"Don't be such an *idiot!* Even if that stone *was* the way, it was lost in Quaunatilcó. You don't want to go back *there!*"

Callie turned to look downhill. The others were straggling up across the trampled field. She spoke urgently, lowly. "We *got* to get Lincoas and them loose. Let go of me. Please! Before everybody in the world gets here. Don't you see?" she stammered self-consciously. "If w-we don't try to stop those speckled kings from hurting Abáloc, it means we don't care, and if we don't care, m-maybe we'll get to be like them." As the words spilled out, the haunting sense of unseen snowy shapes blew away, and she felt suddenly free and sure. "I *got* to go. The way back is through the stone. And if it was here to start with, along with Erilla's stuff, it had to've been buried with her, right? And that means it has to be here still."

Liss blinked, confused. "You mean somebody had to carry it back from Quaunatilcó to Abáloc?" But then, she thought, no matter how often someone touched it, it would always take them back to Abáloc, to Erilla. . . . She dropped to her hands and knees and wriggled after Callie.

"Yo! Wait a minute! What gives?" Mary Lou stumbled on the pile of earth. Kneeling, she caught at Liss's coattail. "Follow-the-leader's over. Enough's enough." She stuck her head in.

Sandy and Marie knelt beside her, breathless, steadying each other.

"Do you s'pose Callie's flipped her wig?" Sandy asked.

"I think they're *both* ready for the funny farm," Erna gasped out. She came trailing after Teeny. "I give up. I'm gonna take this stuff over to Mrs. Washburn at the fancy church. Just lemme catch my breath."

She put a hand on Teeny's shoulder as Teeny collapsed against Marie. The chain was completed in the same second that Callie, groping in the dark, touched the stone.

All seven disappeared.

Fifteen minutes later, Harry, Pooch, Eddie, and Ralph came up along the cemetery wall and into the empty wood at the point farthest from Ridgeview and the Tapp house. They had lost Jack Penrod easily and came the long way around, picking up two shovels in the Hagedorns' garage and borrowing another spade and a flashlight from Mr. Douglass at the nursery. Harry had lured them with tales of treasure, describing the rich tribute the girls had seen buried with Tepollomis. And they had come "for a laugh." But there *was* a mound in the wood, and bare of snow, at that. They grew quiet with a nervous eagerness, wanting the treasure to be there but fearing that if one part of the story were true, so would all the rest be.

"If there *is* anything, we really oughtn't touch it," Pooch said. "Scientists who investigate this kind of stuff always want to know how it's arranged and all that. You know— 'Don't disturb the evidence.'"

Harry climbed the slope at the mound's end, and they followed. Ten yards along, he stopped beside a thick-trunked maple and looked up through its branches.

"This looks like it must be the tallest one along this end. I could see in the field glasses it was right on a kind of bump like this."

He paced a straight line west from the tree and found that the ground fell away slightly unevenly there, as if once there had been an indentation in the bank. The boys scrambled down after him. They dug at that point, at the mound's base.

Harry had calculated to himself that the blue-green stones were somehow the way but that Erilla's was too risky. If Tepollomis's stone—the one the girls had seen at his burial—had the same power, it would take them back to an earlier Abáloc, and he could explain the letters to Erilla and see if the words they had come up with made any sense after all. Or could he? He frowned, watching the others dig. The idea of time was so confusing. Erilla hadn't known the writing. So he, Harry, who did know it now, hadn't told her. His stomach tightened. So why go? Why stick your neck out? But then again: say he did tell her this time. Did that mean what had happened when they were there before would be erased or changed? *Could* you undo anything? His head whirled. Could things unhappen? If Erilla and Tepollomis recovered the *Book of the Kings* and learned where their ancient city under the mountain lay, why . . . they might just *go* there. Leave the village to Neolin and Cibotlán and go. Tepollomis wouldn't be killed. They wouldn't be buried here. There would be no mound, no chambers, no treasure.

"And we'd either be stuck on their side, or we'll find ourselves standing here with shovels wondering what the heck we were doing. Unless we were right back before it all started."

"What're you mumbling?" Eddie panted.

"Come on, Rivers. This was your idea." Ralph pulled his muffler off and stuffed it in his pocket.

"We hit a dead end," Pooch called. His shovel chinked against rock.

It was not a dead end. Uncovered, the obstruction proved to be a large, flat stone, roughly triangular, leaning back at an angle parallel to the mound's slope. Using the shovels as levers, they pried it free. The dark hole of the passage opened behind it.

"Well, here goes nothing," Harry said. He took a deep breath. "You men better wait a minute and then come in."

"Oh, no you don't!" Pooch objected. "You got something up your sleeve. I saw you stick that alphabet stuff in your pocket! Why should you get all the fun?"

Ralph agreed, hiding his misgivings. "Glom onto him, Pucci. I bet he thinks he's gonna get us down that hole and spook us."

"*I* know." Eddie grinned, a little shakily. "He's gonna get us in there and tell us it's a tunnel into the graveyard."

"Six of one and half a dozen of the other," Harry cracked wryly.

They followed him in.

13

The forest hillside was cool and deep and silent, an April-green world in a green light. The sun seemed as distant as if they walked on the bottom of the sea, but its light through the new leaves shimmered with the breeze as it will with the sea's surge. Nothing was familiar, not the thick-rooted giants of trees or the deep silence behind the raucous calls of the flocks of green birds that darted like schools of fish through the shadows. Not even the flowers carpeting the aisles among the trees with blue and yellow.

Eddie knelt. "It looks like violets, man. Only there are *zillions!*"

Ralph spread his fingers wide, as if they might be antennae for finding a bearing in the strangeness. "Not that we ought to know or anything," he said tightly, "but what happened? Am I outa my *skull?* Where are we? What . . . kind of place *is* this?"

Harry bridled. "I *told* you to stay back. You wanted to come. I'd've come without you, but now you're stuck with me." He stalked off down the hill with more confidence than he felt. They would really get spooked if they knew he had no idea where they were.

Pooch and Ralph looked at each other in alarm and dismay.

"Sure," Pooch snapped, in a resentful tone very unlike him. "But how were we supposed to know that it was gonna land us—well, here? Wherever this is."

"You can un-zap us, can't you?" Ralph yelled after Harry.

Eddie had followed behind, looking thoughtful. Now he pushed past the two white boys, catching up with Harry and swinging him around.

"You gotta admit this is pretty weird, man. OK, so we thought you were spinnin' some wild Texas-size fairy tale. Who wouldn't? Now we're here. OK. I'm with you. But I got an idea if Pooch and Raf don't like it, they can't exactly lump it neither. You *tell* us, man."

Harry shrugged, reluctantly admitting that since they were not in Abáloc itself, he hadn't a glimmer where they might be. Privately, he was terrified enough of being lost in this wild land to wonder what would happen if he just up and threw the blue stone away. But if the thing worked so unpredictably, it might not land them home again . . .

"Hsst! Shut up, men!" Ralph gestured to them and froze.

A laugh rang out through the greenwood like a silver bell in a summer's wind. It shattered the mood of distrust and resentment that had woven shadows among the four boys and drew them downhill after it.

From a high ledge overlooking a broad clearing at the edge of a stream, the boys saw the encampment. It had a ramshackle, temporary look. Everywhere there were baskets, full or nearly so. Some held herbs, greens, or flowering plants carefully packed around with earth. Others were deeper, more tightly woven, and lined with pitch so that they could be filled with water. Several young men and women sat along the stream, trailing their hands in the pools. It was from among these that the laughter came, for as the boys watched, a swift hand swept up from the water with a large trout held fast, and the fisherman's companions cheered. The fish were placed in the woven water jars that stood in the cool shallows. From their hidden vantage point, the boys could see this and also the two young women who worked at gutting and skinning squirrels, red, gray, and black, from a heap between them. They salted the meat and placed it in special water jars, salting and kneading the skins before spreading them out on grass mats to dry. A young buck deer hung from a tree near the clearing's edge; and even as the boys watched, two young men brought in another, slung from a carrying pole. They were handsome people, small, brown-skinned, dark-haired, and though some were blue-eyed, most were not. They wore simple garments of blue and brown much like those Harry remembered from Abáloc. He backed away from the ledge and beckoned the others to follow.

"Tepollomis! Lincoas!"

The cry went up from the stream and clearing the moment the boys appeared. They had made an embarrassing amount of noise so that no one would take them for spies.

Tepollomis came through the trees, carrying a throwing spear and a handful of woven string snares. Lincoas and the others were not far behind, bows in hands, arrows nocked and ready. If they faltered, it was for amazement and not a lack of courage.

"Lincoas! Don't you know me?"

But, of course, he did not. Harry realized with a sinking sensation that recognition was still to come, in Quaunatilcó. Tepollomis was yet to die; Erilla had not taken the book from its hiding place; and Lincoas and these others would be captured by raiders from Cibotlán. He should not have come. There was no point in teaching the lost writing to these people. These would never live to see the book.

Lincoas stepped out from the circle of watchers. He was shorter than his father, but held himself more proudly, with more assurance. "You know my name, Black One, but I have never seen your like. How is it you should know me?"

"Gently, gently," Tepollomis warned. He plucked at his son's cloak. "We must have a care. These may be emissaries sent from Cibotlán to ensnare us by a trick. Or they may be some devilish deception of the mind. For who has seen such skins—night-dark and ghost-pale—on human souls? Be gentle, my son, and wary."

Lincoas looked at them sharply. "I guess rather that they come from some far place. A squirrel is a squirrel, no matter what the color of his pelt." He gestured toward the heap of snared animals and then folded his arms. "Come, tell us. Who are you? What is your business here in our gathering grounds if you are not from the encroachers, from Cibotlán?"

"You've got to look out for them," Harry said, in an agony of uncertainty. "They're after you. And if I show you how to figure out Erilla's book, how are you going to get word to her if they jump you all out here in the sticks? Next time we meet, it'll be too late for all that. You'll—"

"Erilla? You speak of my queen?" Tepollomis drew closer. "How come you to know my Erilla? And how dare you speak of a 'book' as hers? The knowledge of such things is forbidden to those who would remain pure of heart."

"Simple of head, you mean!" Harry was rude in his desperation. "*Please.* Just *listen.*"

Tepollomis would have nothing to do with the strange figures that Harry and Pooch scratched in the earth, not even when a fascinated Lincoas translated the full inscription that Harry read out as *The Moon under the Mountain: the First of the Five Books of the Kings of Abáloc*. Harry explained Queen Erilla's hope that the book would reveal the way to Abáloc's ancient refuge and citadel, the City of the Moon under the Mountain.

"Magic," Tepollomis muttered. "No good can come of it. The Serpent oracle warned our forebears that from such magic springs all discontent."

"Aye, discontent, and all wisdom and growing," whispered Ola, a dark-skinned girl with startling blue eyes. "Come, Hari! Give each of us a sound and a sign to take home to Erilla."

Lincoas agreed. The encampment was an hour south and east of Abáloc, and so they dared not delay the trek home for long. Harry's objection, that they must learn the letters there and then because he knew that they had not—*would* not—return to Abáloc with Tepollomis, only confused everyone. But if Harry, Pooch, and the others refused to come to Abáloc, Ola's plan was best. There was no time for all of them to learn so many strange signs and sounds as these. But each could learn one and later, as Lincoas pointed out, they could share among themselves what each had learned.

"Perhaps there will be tales of great adventure in that book, and of all the travels of our people?" Lincoas's eyes shone. "And will it tell the sayings of the oracles that there were in the old days?"

"It might better leave them out," Harry muttered, thinking that it was through oracles that earlier Neolins managed to manipulate these folk. "Here, now this is the first." He pointed to the ⏻ sign with his stick.

In a moment Harry and Pooch had divided the alphabet between them and set to work with the young people who crowded eagerly around, but not all of them were allowed to stay. Some, Tepollomis insisted, must return to keeping watch against the party of Sun Men they had glimpsed earlier in the day, to the south. Eddie tagged along, armed with a borrowed spear, and Ralph drifted toward a downstream pool where several children near his own age had returned to their fishing. They taught a delighted Ralph how to tickle and stroke a trout's belly, soothing it until he could lift it out of the water and into one of the large wicker jars. Tepollomis himself paced the clearing, ordering the completion of tasks and the securing of baskets, giving a kind word here and encouragement there, but worrying all the while. Harry, doggedly repeating the sound, could feel him fretting, moving, advising, with concern but with neither direction nor decision.

"No, no!" Tepollomis protested at last. "This delay is foolhardy. We have never tarried so long at a gathering place. It comes to me that such talk of a *Book of the Kings* —a book no one of us has seen—and of magical signs is but a poor distraction only our enemies would have reason to offer us. What reason do strange children have to be our friends? They must accompany us to Abáloc, where Ayacas and Neolin may advise us. I cannot decide alone, and already soldiers from the Seventh City of Cibotlán may be circling us. They will take in tribute all that we have gathered today, to prove to us once more their strength and our weakness. Come, my children! Come to Neolin and Ayacas."

"Neolin! But he's a traitor!" Harry pushed forward. "He *is.* Quanohtsín owns him. They have him under their big fat thumb because he wants to rule Abáloc for them when you're dead."

There was a shocked silence. Tepollomis's kindness and anxiety were eclipsed by indignation and an unthinking anger that seemed to fill him and leave no room for reason. "Neolin is of Wise Blood. Our people follow his counsel as they followed the counsel of his fathers before him. None but an enemy would slander our Wise Men! Bind them, and erase these wicked sounds from your hearts." With his foot he swept the letter-signs from the dusty earth.

The young men moved reluctantly, but Harry found himself pinioned from behind, and Pooch with him. Ralph and Eddie had disappeared. Harry struggled, but it was useless. Even if he could reach the blue-green stone in his pocket, what could he do with Eddie and Raf gone? He couldn't leave them here. There was much bustle and confusion as baskets were slung from carrying poles and signals blown on a great seashell horn for the scouts to come in. Harry could have wept. If only he had minded his own business. If he got out of this hole, he would make a sign that said just that and hang it on his bedroom wall. Pooch had a dazed, bemused look, as if he had decided that it were all a dream.

There was no answering note from the scouts—only what might have been a distant cry and a sound like a buck in flight, crashing downhill through the underbrush.

"Hurry!" Tepollomis helped the last of the girls to secure the carrying strap of her basket. "Hai! Do not wait for us. *Run!*"

It was a terrified, wild-eyed Eddie who burst into the clearing a moment later. The scouts had been set upon and killed when they resisted. The tattooed warriors had held back at the sight of Eddie and his strange clothing. When they hesitated, he had managed to get away.

The clearing dissolved into chaos. Ralph dropped from the tree he had shinnied up a few moments before and snatched up a fish spear. It was Lincoas who had the presence of mind to cut the thongs that bound Harry and Pooch. There were too few weapons, and as these were being handed out, the Sun Men were upon them.

Afterward, Harry was to remember only a wild kaleidoscope of sounds and colors—a strange, ululating battle cry;

140

girls and young men felled by strange, whirling weapons, cloth tubes filled with sand and wielded at the end of long strings; Lincoas firing arrows steadily; Tepollomis using his spear as knife and quarterstaff until he fell, wounded with a long red-feathered arrow. The noise was horrible. Everyone moved in a dreadful slow motion. Harry found a spear and stood over Tepollomis, but his strength was not much against grown men. He saw Eddie drop, hit from behind, and Ralph lying back against a tree with an arrow clean through him.

"The stone!" Pooch cried out. "The *stone*, you dumbhead!"

Harry's arm was hurt, but he managed somehow to defend himself left-handedly, and groped in his pocket for the stone. He dropped it, despairing, at Tepollomis's side.

14

It was night or seemed at first to be. They were tangled in a darkness thick enough almost to touch or swim in. It swarmed.

"*Skeeters!*" Liss slapped at her cheek.

"You drug me down your old hole!" Erna sputtered. "And my package is torn. That sour old Mrs. Washburn is gonna *kill* me."

"I don't know why you all needed to come," Callie snapped. "I sure didn't mean you to."

As their eyes grew accustomed to the dimness, it became clear that though they might be, figuratively speaking, in a hole, they were in a very real, dank, mosquito-infested forest. Marie's wail of terror got stuck on a hiccup, and she could not stop choking until Erna banged her on the back.

Sandy sneezed violently and hastily covered her mouth. Gnats and mosquitoes swarmed around their noses and mouths so thickly that even the shallowest breathing in and out was risky.

"Cover your face and breathe through your mitten," Liss wheezed. "Or tie a scarf around."

"Look!" Teeny's small voice came through her muffler. "It's light up that way." She began to run.

"Slow up, Teeny. Mind where you put your feet," Liss yelled. "It feels kind of squushy, and I hear water somewheres." She stumbled after Teeny toward the faint glow of light ahead in the dimness.

"They're chewin' at my *eyelids*," Marie shrieked.

"Hold on, everybody." Callie stopped and, stooping, scraped away at the leaf carpet. "Use mud. My grandma told me that once. All over your hands and face, thick and smeary."

It helped a little, though breathing was still a problem. The girls ran awkwardly in their heavy clothing and came after a little while to a trail, narrow, but too straight and purposeful to be a deer trail. Following its course, climbing almost imperceptibly, they came to the light, a thinning of the forest where pale shafts of sunlight fell through the woven roof. It was a forest unlike that which Callie and Liss had seen before. It was completely alien in its strangeness, like something glimpsed in the far deeps of time. Tall, thick trunks soared, bare of branches for fifty feet or more, to where, high overhead, their leafy crowns were matted together with vines and creeping plants. The understory trees trailed long beards of moss and were woven together with canopies of creepers. The dense underbrush was laced with crisscrossing, aimless tracks, and giant spider webs glistened in the sunfall. At least here the brush was lower, the insects fewer.

"Oh, Callie, where *are* we?" Liss was bewildered and angry. "Why'd you have to come back here? It's none of our business." She wiped her nose with the back of her hand, smearing the mud in a wide streak.

"I know." Callie had an awful feeling, a small, cold lump weighing heavily below her heart. "It was just I couldn't bear us getting off, and Lincoas and all them getting carved up, or whatever they do. I couldn't bear it. But something's gone wrong. I don't see how. I thought if the stone was back in the chamber, why, it would take us to where we left off. Or back to Abáloc, so *they* could help Lincoas. If it was the stone that took us, you see, we could always escape home like last time."

The others listened, speechless, bewildered. Liss stamped her foot angrily. "But, Cal, don't you see? The stone *was* back in the mound. That means somebody *did* bring it back from Quaunatilcó. Maybe Lincoas. How else would Erilla get it back?"

"I figured maybe *we* brought it. Or got Lincoas loose so that he could. I mean, like the stone might bring us to where we left off in Quaunatilcó. You know? And if they were going to take us all to that other place . . . the one with the sloshy name? Tushcloshán? Why, we'd have time to think up some trick to get Lincoas and his friends loose of the Seven Kings. . . ." Callie's voice trailed off helplessly.

Liss frowned up into the lush, moss-hung gloom of the forest. Spanish moss, like in pictures of . . . "Maybe we *are* on the way to Tushcloshán. Didn't they say it was way off to the south?" She shivered. "It's sure jungly enough, even if it isn't hot."

The words stirred in Callie a long-forgotten memory. Grandma. Grandma telling stories of the Mississippi Delta. There had been one about an old man who lived by an ancient, haunted forest—woven dark and dank and chill—where no one hunted, because dogs wouldn't set foot in it unless they were beaten and forced in.

"I guess we're somewheres south, all right. But it looks like our old stone's got discombobulated, maybe because of having to bring such a load of us. We missed connections somehow. *If* it was to find Lincoas we got plonked down here, that is. Maybe that all sounds dumb, but that's what I guessed—that we were *supposed* to. I guess it doesn't figure, though, 'cause we didn't have to come. We can go back right this minute if you all want to."

That, everyone understood. Mud-faced and frightened, they crowded around, taking hands in a circle, an instinctive ritual of reassurance in the tangled deeps of the wilderness. Callie fished the stone from her pocket and threw it on the ground.

Nothing happened. Two black squirrels chased up an ash tree. The soft background chatter and rustling of invisible animals went on. The sloggy ground made gentle sucking sounds as Erna shifted weight from one foot to another. Callie picked up the stone and turned it over in her hand, frightened. She had a strange feeling that its power was not in itself but in Erilla's heart—and that blind power, reaching out, had drawn them here. But why here? Why this place?

"Maybe if you threw it outside the circle?" Liss whispered. "Everybody concentrate."

Teeny was not listening. She dropped Sandy's hand and turned away from the circle. "You guys," she said. "Unless the skeeters have numbed my nose, I think I smell food cooking. Sweet potatoes and something. Is it a mirage?"

It was sweet potatoes. Half a mile beyond, on higher ground but still in the darkness of deep forest, the trail led them to the stream they had heard from the first. Keeping together, they climbed to a rock ledge overlooking both trail and stream and followed it to a point where, peering down through the bushes, they could see a clearing with four or five thatched lean-tos and two busy fire circles. Forty or more men squatted by the fires or in groups near the shelters, eating and laughing. They fell silent when from far away, high up the trail, a horn blast dimly sounded. An officer came out from under the shelter of the ledge to answer it with a long deep note on a great conch shell.

Callie and Liss touched each other, signaling their relief. Perhaps they were not lost after all. Motioning the others to follow, they crept along the ledge, dropping to the trail and running only after they were well out of earshot.

"That was one of Cibotlán's outposts," Liss explained breathlessly. "They must be why we're here."

"Just so long as we don't meet ourselves comin' down the trail! That's all I ask," Callie panted, only half laughing. "If it's two black kids and some nut with no coat on, roaring like a stuck elephant, I quit."

As they climbed, the forest opened out, the air grew clearer and sweeter, and the stream splashed among rocks. Suddenly, unexpectedly, they were in a small valley between two wooded hills—a sweet-smelling lost garden where large-leaved magnolias stood tall among slippery elms and silver-bell trees, where mountain laurel and camellias brightened the hillsides, and where the ground was covered with yellow violets, fern, and saxifrage. The girls drank the cold, sweet water greedily from their cupped hands.

Refreshed, they climbed to the crest of the higher hill. There, on the ridge beyond, they saw what—so it seemed to Liss and Callie—they had come to meet: a long, winding caravan moving at a quick pace.

"Ssst! Eagle Eyes!"

Erna was pushed to the front, but she could tell them only that the litters were like hammocks and those who rode in them were too swathed in robes or blankets to tell whether they were tattooed or not.

"Then we got to snag one of them 'n find out," said Callie. "Any ideas?"

"You got to be kidding," Mary Lou ventured. The others took it quite calmly. The preposterous had begun to sound only reasonable. "Well, there's all those vines down below,"

147

she said in sudden abandon. "Could we booby-trap the path?"

Sandy had a knife, with which they cut lengths from the trailing creepers. Callie and Marie worked at tying single knots at each end to serve as grips. Erna would not abandon her package, so she and it were to be posted just below the small valley, at the edge of the darkness. As the last sweet oasis before the glooming lowlands, the little valley should tempt the bearers to slow their pace, and Erna was to bird-whistle a warning when they came in sight. At the last minute before Erna moved out, a newly adventurous Teeny thought to ask what was in the package. With a gleam in her eye, she tore the rip in the paper wider despite Erna's protests.

"I knew it! Look, everybody. Choir robes." She grinned. "If we put them on, Erna can't lose them, and we'll look wonderfully ghosty." Erna was not very happy about it, but she had to admit that it was not a bad idea. As there were twelve robes, she made each of them wear two. She did not take one herself, for it would be to her advantage to be as invisible as possible, since she would not have the cover of the deep forest. "It's no good your sayin' you'll steam like clams," she warned. "You wear both. My mother'd skin me if I lost 'em."

Erna trotted back up to the thinning trees below the clearing, and the others moved down into the darkness to lay a series of shaggy vines across the track. At Erna's signal they hid in the undergrowth. The long caravan passed at a trot: twenty-odd litters swaying through the gloom. As the last approached, Callie and Liss raised the vine that lay across the path between them, held it taut, and let it go at the moment the lead bearer tripped. Liss whipped the vine out of sight, and while the bearers regained the rhythm of their stride, both girls darted ahead, parallel to the trail.

Sandy and Marie tripped the first bearer a second time in the same way, and then Mary Lou and Callie repeated the trick a few yards beyond. Wary, but not particularly alarmed, the bearers slowed and soon had fallen considerably behind the others. Quickly, the girls moved ahead to the last vine. With two at each end, they raised it to just below knee level, snubbing it around a young tree on each side. The bearer went down with a crash and a curse at the same moment a transformed Teeny leaped into the trail before him, flapping white wings and wailing softly. Bearers and guard broke and ran, pursued, they thought, by demons.

"Here, quick!" Callie darted to the heap in the trail where a dazed young man sat in a tangle of netting and poles. "Gimme your knife, Sandy."

Liss passed the knife to her, then worked to free the poles. "Abáloc? Are you from Abáloc?" She panted. "Do you know Lincoas?"

He pulled the neck of his robe down from around his ears to whisper, "Moon and stars! You are not ghosts? I am Lincoas. Who are . . ." He stared at the circle of mud-dark faces and then pointed in amazement at Callie. "You? Why, you were with Hari, my young friend Hari, in Quaunatilcó! Yet you were not with him when first I met him. And how did you come to be here? Who are you?"

"Introductions later." Callie slashed at the braided thong binding his hands. "Bring your ropes, you guys." She pulled him after her off the trail.

"Erna? Where's Erna?" Liss looked around frantically. "Oh, good. Hey, somebody! Chuck that hammock in the bushes. Sandy? Grab the other pole. These'll bring them down harder than any old vine."

They tripped up the party of six bearers who came back to investigate. Without lanterns the men were at a disadvantage until their eyes could grow more accustomed to the gloom, and they were terrorized by the white shapes flitting and moaning in the darkness. Panic spread up the line, and before the officer in charge could light his lantern, a number of the young men and women from Abáloc had been freed to join in the melee with great gusto. Callie, in the midst of cutting one girl's bonds, suddenly straightened. When did he ever see Harry before Quaunatilcó?

Lincoas was too busy to interrupt with questions. In a moment he had tumbled the officer into the dark stream and, warned by Liss about the reinforcements only half a mile away, was urging his people to the high ground.

They did not stop until, deep in the rolling hills, they came upon another small green valley, safely distant from the trail. The weary girls were helped along, pulled and pushed by friendly hands. Teeny rode the last mile on the back of a strong young man.

"You have saved us from the knife," Lincoas said when he had drunk from the stream and caught his breath. "They were taking us to the great southern city of Tushcloshán, to the great feast, where we were to be sacrificed. With great pomp and splendor." He snorted. "It is an honor we are happy to refuse. But how did you find us? Where is Hari?"

"How did you know his name?" Callie and Liss spoke together. "How could you?"

Lincoas was bewildered. "But he told us himself, on the day we were taken prisoner. It was he who told us of the City of the Moon. Surely he has spoken of it? Though he was hurt and his friend—one of the pale-skinned boys— sorely wounded, somehow they escaped. But his friend cannot have lived. How is it you do not know these things? And how do you come to be at this place? And where from? When first we saw such as you, there were but four, and all were boys. Then in Quaunatilcó, as in a dream, I saw Hari again, and these two others." He pointed to Callie and Liss. "And now—dream upon dream—we are saved by girl-children from Tushcloshán and the death that waited us there. You do not look like goddesses. Are you ghosts? Or Moon Beings?"

Callie felt queasy, as if the ground had shifted under her feet with each question. He was talking nonsense. She saw Liss's face go a pasty white beneath the smeary mud and followed her glance. Only then did she see the rude medallion one of the young women was fashioning from a chip of fir bark with Sandy's knife. Across it she had cut her name: L **8O**

"We've got to get home. This minute," Callie gasped. She hitched up the muddy white robes and fumbled in her pocket.

Lincoas stared at the blue-green stone where it lay in the palm of her hand. Then, without a word, he unknotted a corner of the hem of his long tunic and drew out a stone exactly like it.

"Where'd you get *that?*"

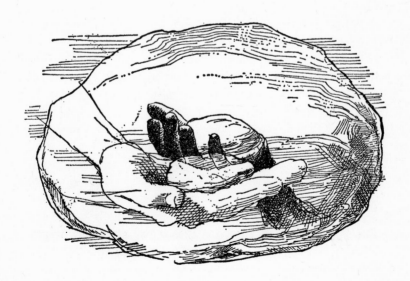

It was identical, down to the faint scratch straggling across one side.

"You gave it me. Rather, you dropped it. In Quaunatilcó."

As they watched, palm to palm, the two stones shimmered, blurred, and became one. Frightened, Lincoas dropped it, then stooped to pick it up again. The stone was smooth and solid in his hand, but the strange children were gone. He passed a shaky hand across his eyes.

"What are we waiting for?" he cried at last. "It is a long road north to Abáloc! And who knows how far the road to the City of the Moon under the Mountain?"

15

"There isn't any hole in his coat, you guys."
Ralph stood blinking in the snow, a hand pressed to his side. "I'm OK, I tell you. Quit pawing. I'm OK." Miraculously, it seemed he was. "What do you want me to do? Take my clothes off in a snowstorm?"

"Let's go down to Mr. Douglass's," Sandy proposed, always practical. "You can take them off there."

"Oh, come *on!* You think I'm gonna take my shirt off in front of a bunch of girls?"

"Don't be stupid, Hagedorn. We seen you lots of times in your swim trunks."

"That's different. Besides, there's *no* hole through my ribs." He brushed the subject aside. "What's old Erna moaning and groaning about?"

Erna was moaning about the choir robes, which were hopelessly rumpled and stained. "I was s'posed to use the money from Mrs. Washburn for our turkey. How'm I s'posed to go home without the turkey? You tell me that. I only got ten cents in my pocket. Ten cents! That's not even a good down payment on a chicken leg." She began to cry.

"Oh, for crumbs' sake, woman." Harry groaned. "Now she's got the hiccups. Somebody thump on her. How much you got, Callie? I got a quarter."

Altogether, they could manage half of a respectable turkey, and Pooch vouched for the other half. They could get it at Pucci's Grocery and not have to worry about closing time. The lead-colored sky gave no clue whether it was five o'clock or nearer three. Liss and Harry's watches had stopped, and Teeny's read an improbable ten-thirty.

"But what about the robes?" Erna snuffled. "Old Mrs. Washburn's so picky. She'll be in a snit if she has to wait till tomorrow."

"Don't worry." Liss collected the robes. "She doesn't really need them till tomorrow afternoon, for the Thanksgiving service. I'll phone and say you had to give them to me to bring over in the morning. She won't grump if she knows they're practically next door. Mama and Mrs. Calvert and I can get them done up in time. Here, give me that one."

Callie handed over the last of the robes. The snow was falling in earnest, large, thick flakes that had already blurred smooth the trampled field and drifted in the wind. Liss hurried off in the direction of Ridgeview, and the others scurried to camouflage the two tomb passages, packing them with leaves and branches.

As Liss came to the fence just inside the wood, the wind died and the snow fell more slowly, silently. No wind. And yet she felt as if she were struggling against just such a force—leaning into and pushing against it, moving slowly, strangely, as if the air itself were heavy, thick, and sticky as molasses. It was stronger the closer she came to the house; and then suddenly it was gone, as if some presence had drawn back to let her pass. She ran.

According to the big, old-fashioned timepiece on the wall of Mr. Douglass's little showroom, it was half-past four. The children peered in at the steamy window and, seeing no Mr. Douglass, trooped around the building to the greenhouse side and in the back door.

"House Rule: coats off so no one catches his death going out again." In the steamy warmth of the geranium section, the small, grizzle-haired old man who had spoken stirred away at a large enameled pot on a hot plate. Turning, he eyed the children with a frightening glare that was alarming even when you were used to it, as most of them were.

"Two, three . . . six . . . eight, *ten*. Against all the rules! The house doesn't have ten cups. Gentlemen will have to use marmalade jars."

Eddie sniffed ecstatically. "Hot chocolate! Bad, man!"

"How'd you know we'd be coming?" Ralph shrugged off his coat and hung it on one of the two-dozen nails studding the back of the door.

"What goes up must come down. House Rule. What I ask myself is, since it is not likely they were paying polite house calls, what were they up to? Prospecting in the graveyard, no. Callie, marmalade jars!" As she scurried into the next room, he held up a warning hand to the others. "No, no explanations. Life is a pool. A man gets plunked in the middle, and it's dog-paddle or drown. As you were. I'll piece it together as you go. Here, Agostino. Wrap yourself around a cookie. Made 'em this morning: Nasty Turtiums, sugar, flour, marge, ground-up almonds, egg, and violets." He thrust a plate and mug at Teeny. "Eat it—don't goggle at it, woman. Sugar violets'd cost you a couple dollars for a tiddly little box if you was to buy 'em. And you wouldn't find 'em any nearer'n Pittsburgh, neither."

When Teeny finished the cookie with a smile and did not rush for the nearest sink, the boys passed the plate.

The cookies were strange but surprisingly good, and the hot chocolate was superb. Mr. Douglass stirred a spoonful of marmalade into his own, but no one copied that. There was a limit to adventure.

"What I don't understand is the *time*," Harry said. "The first time we were gone three days, and it only took five minutes. This time we were gone two-three hours, and it took two whole hours."

Callie nodded. "I bet we weren't there for more'n an hour, but it took us *more* than two."

Marie frowned. "It sounds like your stones are wearing down, you know?"

Mr. Douglass choked on his orange chocolate. "I give up," he sputtered, brushing at the droplets on his plaid shirtfront. "Now me, I can walk in on a movie show fifteen minutes before the end and get right into the swing of it. Point of pride, you might say. Never at a loss. But would you mind runnin' back over that last at low speed? I think you lost me back at the first curve."

They would not have told any other adult for fear of sounding like idiots, but Mr. Douglass was different. If he thought you sounded like an idiot, he said so. And then he would say, "Go on, then. Spit it all out. No sense leaving it inside to curdle your brains. I'm all ears." Besides, there was much that they had not told each other up on the snowy Edge. The deciphering of the alphabet and the battle and ambush were recounted blow-by-blow. If the girls were impressed into wide-eyed silence by the account of the boys' struggle against overpowering odds, the boys were in stitches at the girls' talent for guerrilla ambush. Ralph even consented to pull up his shirt to let everyone see that there wasn't a mark on him.

"But it really felt like . . . like dying," he said with a shiver. "Another minute, and I might not've gotten back."

Everyone sobered.

"Well, we got it all cleared up," Harry said. "So long as Lincoas gets home, they can throw Neolin out and move somewhere else."

"The City of the Moon under the Mountain," Callie murmured.

"But we'll never know for sure what happened," Pooch objected. "What if that book didn't help them after all?"

"That's the breaks." Harry tried to sound flippant but was not very successful. He bit his lip and tried to push that worry away, but it was persistent. "I know. But it *is* all over. They're *all* dead now. And we're out of it. If, like Marie says, the stones have been getting weaker, they're too dangerous to use. We might get truly trapped. Or maybe they won't work at all now. Maybe they just worked, well, when we were *needed*. You're right, though. It would be nice to know . . ."

"Ah, you don't want much, do you?" said Mr. Douglass. He shrugged. "Who ever knows how *anything* will come out? You talk like things get tied up in neat little packages. 'All cleared up,' he says. That makes time sound like a desk full of pigeonholes. I'm not saying I understand all this jabber about kings and lost cities, but if there's any truth to it, you've likely not heard the end of it. 'Now that's over, stick a label on it.' Is that the kind of museum you say you're puttin' together down to Pucci's? Well, it don't work that way. Though it's pretty hard to say just how it does work. Time's funny. A minute can be longer for one man than for the fellow standin' right next him. And time is different here among the tomatoes and azaleas from what it is down at S and S in the blooming mill, or at the open hearth where your dad works, Harry Rivers. No. Don't be too sure you're finished with whatever it is. Things die down, but they're like to keep right on underneath. Seems I read somewheres once, 'The past is never dead. It's not even past.' A smart man wrote that." He munched thoughtfully on another cookie.

Mary Lou blinked. "How's that again?"

"And the moon is made of Mozzarella," Pooch cracked. He took his marmalade jar to the sink and washed it out. "He's pulling our collective leg."

"Yeah." Harry followed him. "Past is past." Of course time was relative, but over *was* over.

"Done is done!"

"And gone is gone," sang Erna, gathering up the cups. "I gotta be gone turkey-wards."

Marie and Teeny whispered together. "But today will be yesterday tomorrow!" they warbled idiotically.

"None of that! Keep it neat and clean." Ralph clasped a potted pelargonium in his arms and waltzed it down to the chrysanthemums and back up through the rows of shrubbery in tubs. "Here we go 'round the barberry bush, the barberry bush," he panted, suiting the action to the words.

"This is the day we wash our irons!"

"This is the day we clothe our dogs . . ."

"So early i-in the morn-ing!"

". . . sew our toes . . ."

The song was lost in breathless laughter. Gradually, cups were dried and put away, a broken marmalade jar swept up, and in a last burst of high silliness coats were put on backward. Everyone had to have help in buttoning up.

"Confusion, confusion!" Mr. Douglass repeated mournfully. Closing the door behind them at last, he threw up his hands. "Take their tall tales a bit serious-like, and they go all skittery-flap. Back is front and up is down. *Not* a new House Rule." But he knew it had been their left-footed way of changing the subject, and his curiosity was thoroughly aroused.

158

It seemed strange on the Monday after Thanksgiving to have no school. Miss Langley returned dutifully for a special teachers' meeting at Fourth Street and to pack books, papers, and clothing for a long Christmas vacation in Poole. Because her refrigerator was empty and she had promised lunch to her friend Professor Novak in exchange for his driving her from Poole and back, she and the professor happened into Pucci's shortly before noon.

"No, no, not that one. This one." Mr. Douglass appeared from nowhere to relieve her of one bunch of broccoli and hand her another. "Much fresher. Tighter. Bluer."

"Um . . . thank you." She blinked and managed an introduction. "Mr. Douglass, Professor Richard Novak. But what are you doing here, Mr. Douglass? I thought it was a House Rule: your own chickens, your own eggs, your own vegetables?"

"Mm. Yes. I ran out of chocolate." He reddened, gruffly admitting, "No, that's not strictly true. I came to see the Elephant."

"The . . . *Elephant?*"

"Mm. Blinks very nicely, doesn't she, Professor? You've not been up to see yet, Josie? I was hoping you had the password."

"Up? Password?" She widened her eyes in mock suspense. The professor, on the other hand, was embarrassed, thinking the old man childish or confused, or both.

"Why, your youngsters. Upstairs. A museum, they said." Mr. Douglass stabbed a finger upward toward the ceiling.

"Yah." Mr. Pucci leaned over the meat counter. "All weekend they pound, pound, pound, and I gotta run up every five minutes to be sure they don't put more nails in the walls. Why is it so quiet now, I want to know? Go on up if you want. It'll save me getting a worse charley horse than I got on Saturday."

"Two-O-Six?" Miss Langley stared at the number over the door. The numbers had been painstakingly cut from plywood with a small bandsaw and lacquered an electric blue. "That's my homeroom number," she said, marveling.

Mr. Douglass knocked and stuck his head in. Miss Langley peered over him, and the tall, bearded professor leaned in at the top. "Good morning," they all said rather lamely. "Good heavens!" added the amazed Miss Langley.

The whole class appeared to be there, except for Doris Austin, who couldn't be bothered, and Wally Gowins, who was not on the grapevine. Mel Brown and Eddie Williams were up on chairs screwing small fixtures onto the old picture molding that ran around the room. Beverly Floyd and Sandy polished the wood on two old-fashioned glass-topped biscuit bins while Charlie Baker, biting his lip, tried to cut a pane of glass for the lid of a third from a pane scavenged from the Building Supply. Under one table, Jack Penrod was lettering little cards to go with his Indian collection. Frank Rosen, Harry, and Ralph sat on the floor by the window, swapping sandwiches. Liss, Susie Mossberger, Mary Lou, and Marie were painting on window blinds rolled out on the floor, and Callie was propped in a corner with a book. Tank Sherman, big and black, and even more incorrigibly cheerful than Sandy, stood on a chair in the middle of the room with Jim Toohey up on his shoulders. Jim screwed hundred-watt bulbs into the light fixture as Erna passed them up and took the burned-out twenty-five watters in exchange. Teeny had the desk and a messy box of watercolors to herself and did not look up at the interruption. But a surprised Pooch had and was covered with confusion because there he stood by the desk, twisting Anne Palisser's arm up behind her back to make her return his pastrami sandwich and take back her egg salad. A battered record player provided an exotic accompaniment of drums, guitars, and bells.

"Hey, go on out and knock again," Tommy Mistovich yelled from inside the big display case, where he was arranging an odd assortment of glass and crockery on a brightly painted shelf.

Mr. Douglass obediently pulled the door shut and knocked politely. There was a great rush and scramble, three *wait a minute*'s, and a minor crash, followed by a decorous silence. Pooch opened the door with a flourish.

Library books were stacked on the rainbow-colored stock shelves, and biscuit-box cases were arranged on a yellow door-table. The blinds hung along the wall—unfinished but colorful maps of the Tri-State area. One showed mounds and Indian settlements as well as present-day towns, and another located the many primitive iron furnaces of the settlers, later iron works, and modern steel mills. Paintings of local fish and animals and birds, the extinct and the familiar side by side, were pinned up alongside Teeny's watercolors of a rich, strange primordial forest. The large cases, painted blue and green, contained cups and bowls, from the shell cup and squirrel-rimmed bowl of Abáloc through old wooden ware, two pieces of early Apple Lock glass, and a few rather ugly modern pieces from Seese Pottery. The second shelf held, among many other metal objects, the Abáloc medallion, square nails and spikes, and tiny springs of the finest steel. Shoeboxes of arrowheads and fossils waited to be arranged.

Callie waved an expansive arm and grinned sheepishly. "We're workin' on a new House Rule: 'unpigeonholing.'"

"Some of it's stuff we did for those reports that got postponed," Pooch explained a little apologetically. "Only it's all sort of overlapped . . ."

"Never mind that!" The professor found his voice. "Please . . ." He pushed through to kneel in front of the case and asked rather shakily, "May I?" He slid the door open, touched the shell cup, and gingerly lifted out the squirrel bowl. Shaking his head in bewilderment, he ran his hands over it in a caress and then saw the medallion.

"Where? Where did you get these things?" He turned to the circle of faces.

The children stared. His knuckles were white, and he was trembling with excitement.

16

"**P**lease, honey! Get them out of here." The professor gestured toward the far end of the Edge. "That's a foul-tempered, shrivel-hearted old man over there, and he says he'll lock this site up and wait until Rishanger —he's the big mound expert—until he can come if we don't clear away the trashy kids. Says he won't have them on the property."

"*Richard!*"

"His adjective, not mine." The professor propelled Miss Langley forward with a gentle pressure under her elbow. "They're great kids," he said placatingly, "but we don't need them underfoot all the time, now do we?"

She pulled free and snapped at him. "Apparently not. But then I hadn't thought of digging and sifting buckets of earth as 'being underfoot.' It looked more like 'doing the donkey work' to me."

"But the kids from the college are here to do that now. And for Pete's sake, Josie, keep your voice down. This must be the most important archaeological discovery in this country in years, and *I* don't want to get kicked off the property.

Do you have any idea how many fresh-water pearls we've brought out so far? *Twenty-two gallons!* Hurry up like a good girl. Get those kids away. Here comes old Tapp."

Miss Langley made her way past the surveyors, past the crew hoisting a magnetometer onto the mound to take readings that might indicate the location of other chambered tombs, and past the workmen busy erecting the chain-link fence that was to enclose the entire mound. Archaeologists from West Virginia University and Ohio State seemed to be everywhere, directing student workers, advising photographers, and talking to reporters. The children had withdrawn as far as the cemetery wall and sat in a straggly row atop it, kicking their heels. *She* felt like kicking Richard Novak.

"Is he your boyfriend, Miss Langley?" Mary Lou scowled her disapproval.

Miss Langley thrust her hands deeper into her coat pockets and regarded Mary Lou thoughtfully. "No. No, and if he were, I think I'd fire him." She grinned ruefully. "At the moment he has a one-pigeonhole mind, to borrow everyone's favorite figure of speech. It will wear off. But for now, come along, men! We have been declared redundant and asked to leave."

Several of the girls jumped down from the wall. "You too, Miss Langley?"

The boys were sullen and ready to be very angry. "You don't have to go just because we do," Pooch objected. "We heard old man Tapp. He said we *stole* that stuff."

Harry spoke acidly. "That's *his* good excuse. You can bet if we were all lily-white and talked like butter wouldn't melt and walked two by two in lines like in the olden days, he wouldn't have said it even if it was what he thought."

"I thought treasure was finders-keepers," Callie complained. "Besides, it was Liss's idea to take it away."

"It's all my fault. I never thought Grandpa would mind

so awfully." Liss peered over the cemetery wall. "I'm hiding," she explained. "I snuck across on the other side of the woods and came through the cemetery. Grandpa won't listen to me, and Mama's at work, and I'll just *bust* if I can't tell somebody who can help."

"Tell someone what?"

"The Edge—the mound—it doesn't belong to Grandpa! I tried to tell him, but he won't listen." She danced up and down in an agony of frustration. "When I was at the County Records Office, I . . ."

A loud outcry from the wood shattered their attention.

"Hey! Somebody call a doctor!" A sharp voice rang through the trees.

"A doctor? Oh, dear!" Miss Langley's hand flew to her mouth in alarm. "Oh, dear. Someone's been hurt." She turned and ran.

The children looked at each other in deep disgust. She obviously thought it was her professor or feared so.

"Well," offered Teeny timidly, "he has a nice beard."

"Aah, he's moldy," Jack Penrod pronounced with surprising energy. He kicked at a fallen branch.

"Come on," Harry grumbled. "Let's go down the hill before they send the constable to chase us off. We'll see you later, Liss."

Mr. Douglass flagged down the procession as it straggled past the nursery. "Come along in. In, in, and close the door. We're on television! Channel Nine's canceled my Perry Mason this afternoon. Special news program on the great discovery at Apple Lock. Year in, year out nobody's ever heard of Apple Lock, and now twice in two weeks. At least this seems a happier sort of ruckus; not like the schools closing down. Come along. I moved the TV back to the potting counter."

A studio announcer was speaking, and the children sat on crates and upended flowerpots to watch. ". . . the importance of Monday afternoon's discovery by Professor Richard Novak of Poole College (Harry groaned. *"His* discovery? Oh, man!"*) was quickly recognized by archaeological experts. Scientists from Ohio State, specialists in the Ohio Valley mound cultures, have been in Apple Lock since Tuesday, and a contingent from West Virginia University arrived yesterday. The national news services and *Life* Magazine are on the spot. The ancient mound, which Professor M. P. Renta estimates to be work of the eleventh or twelfth century A.D., is located atop the highest point of Apple Ridge, overlooking the Ohio River."

The announcer's voice droned on, but now the picture was a film of the woods on the Edge, taken from the road on the golf course side. "Despite its impressive view," the voice said, "the property has never been developed. Mrs. Alice Attley, a long-time resident, seen here talking with your reporter, recalls that in her childhood these woods and the field below were rumored to be 'haunted.' Other residents of Ridgeview admit to avoiding the property because of its 'feel.'"

Back in the studio, the announcer smirked.

"You better believe it!" Callie said.

"Certainly," he went on with owlish gravity, "the temperature variations on the site are unusual. Normally, digging at this time of year would be impossible, but a freak localized thaw has allowed archaeologists to make exploratory excavations. Professor Renta of Ohio State is with us in the studio this afternoon. Welcome, Professor Renta."

"Thank you, Jim. Happy to be here."

"Professor, could you tell us something of what you have found so far?"

The professor, looking very professorial, nodded. "Certainly, Jim. I'd be glad to. As this bird's-eye plan will show you, this two-hundred-and-eighty-eight-foot mound is of a shape encountered nowhere else."

A slide drawing flashed on the screen:

"Professor Novak and I believe that, allowing for the erosion of time and the encroachment of the woods, the original shape of the mound would have been something like this . . ."

A second drawing appeared:

"Here," Professor Renta explained, "the point labeled B, is the treasure chamber and its passage. Point A is the second chamber, which apparently contained only simple grave goods. These were discovered by local children, who had no idea of their significance. ("Who says *you* do?" a member of the greenhouse audience muttered.) The portion indicated here by the dotted line seems clearly to be a somewhat later addition, as it is not in harmony with the original design. It is a square, flat-topped shape typical of the temple sites of the sun-worshiping Temple Mound Culture, which superceded those simpler cultures that built mounds for the burial and honoring of the dead . . ."

"That's right," Callie said. "I read that in one of those books. But that means—"

"Hsst! Listen!" Harry ordered.

"This central section may, of course, also contain burials.

That we do not know as yet. However, it seems clear that it did serve some ceremonial function as well. This morning we found, at its very center, and at a depth of only two feet, a large stone slab—very unusual in these circumstances —almost certainly a sacrificial altar. The temple itself would have been built of wood . . ."

"Then Lincoas never got back." Callie felt sick. "Neolin won after all. After all."

Mr. Douglass held his tongue. Tall tales again? But the children seemed genuinely disturbed.

Harry ground his teeth. "It can't be. It *can't* be." He stood and wandered out behind the tomato plants.

The others listened in unhappy silence to the dry, pleasant voice as it went on describing the treasure and answering questions about its value. A single long string of the fresh-water pearls might be worth three or four thousand dollars, but they were even more valuable as artifacts than as pearls.

"To hear them talk, you'd never think live, warm people ever wore those beads or loved Tepollomis before he was just a heap of interesting bones," Callie said resentfully. "Can't they talk about anything but the money?"

It seemed others were interested in the money, too. There was a film sequence showing the erection of the fence ("Look, there we are over on the right!"), and another in which old Senator Tapp described his plans for the treasure: a Conway Tapp III Memorial Foundation Museum at the state capitol in memory of his son and as "an inspiration" to his grandson, Conway Tapp IV. "That boy is going to make this area sit up and take notice one of these days. He's only a little fellow now, but he's got what it takes." Back in the studio, the commentator reported that, despite the Senator's plans, there were rumors that the ownership of the property was not clear. It had been a part of the original Tapp grant made in 1819, but the director of the Ridgeview Cemetery and the Board of Trustees of the Ridgeview Golf Club had hired surveyors to recheck boundary lines.

"How do you like that!" Ralph cracked. "Even the grave-yard's greedy."

A cheerful voice interrupted. "But it isn't going to do them a bit of good. Not a smidge!"

While the bell on the front door was still tinkling, Liss came scurrying back through the showroom, followed by Miss Langley wreathed in smiles, and a tall, lanky over-coated figure swathed in an ugly woolly scarf and earmuffs.

"Mr. Moon!" They recognized the shaggy eyebrows. Mr. Moon was the Superintendent of Schools and, according to Pooch, a sort of cross between the Jolly Green Giant and an absentminded St. Bernard dog.

"Be of good cheer. The cavalry is here!" he boomed.

"It is, it is!" Miss Langley threw her arms around Mr. Douglass and waltzed him through the geraniums and back. "Tell them, Melissa. Oh, justice! Oh, poetry!" She laughed.

Liss plumped down on a crate. Harry reappeared and switched off the television.

"Well, you see—" Liss took a deep breath. "I was doing the County Records Office for our reports. Anyhow, I got this idea: why not see if I could find out something about the Edge? The first bit was easy, because it was part of the first Tapps' farm, like Grandfather says. There weren't any deed transfers or records of that bit being sold off, like there were for the pieces that went for the cemetery or the park or the golf course, and I got awfully bored reading all those catalogues to the records every afternoon, and all the old directory books. So I gave up on the Edge."

"You quit? But what's the good news, then?" Callie was bewildered, and the others echoed her.

"Just wait! Yesterday, Mr. Potts—he's the County Clerk

—explained about tax records and pet licenses and birth certificates and wedding licenses and that kind of stuff." She grinned. "So I asked if I could see my birth certificate, and he showed me. That's when I found it!"

"*What* 'it'?" Teeny prompted.

"A loose sheet out of one of the tax ledgers—a list of all the Ridgeview school tax payments for 1903. It had slipped down from the drawer above, I guess. And there wasn't any—"

Mr. Douglass let out a crow of delight. He saw what was coming.

Mr. Moon nodded. "As Superintendent of Schools, I have access to those tax records. Melissa paid me a visit this morning to ask whether I couldn't check them to see if she was right, and I spent the afternoon at the courthouse doing just that. I found the explanation only an hour ago: in 1893 Senator Tapp's father refused to pay the new school taxes. He was sending his boys to boarding school over east and said that the district could have his piece of wasteland in place of the money if they wished. But he wouldn't pay a penny of school tax. He simply . . . let the Edge go!" Mr. Moon flapped his arms. "I made a beeline for the Ridge and found Melissa and your Miss Langley. They guessed some of you would be here."

"The mound belongs to the *school district?*" Only Eddie Williams managed to find a voice, and his squeaked. "Man-oh-man-oh-man!"

"Isn't it gorgeous?" Miss Langley forgot herself so far as to clap her hands and whirl around like a top, doing a sort of dervish dance in her high boots.

Mr. Douglass could not make himself heard over the hubbub that followed. He could only cover his ears, cast his eyes to the ceiling, and hope fervently that nothing would be broken. All that glass . . . he winced.

It was not long before half of the children had gone home to dinner and to spread the news. Mr. Moon offered to drop Miss Langley off and then to drive Liss back up to Ridgeview, where he hoped to speak with her grandfather.

"Hey, Miss Langley!" Harry suddenly remembered Professor Novak. "What was the accident up there on the Edge? Was somebody hurt?"

She sobered and pulled back her long hair, fastening it with a tie strip from a tomato plant. The clip that usually held it had fallen off in the excitement. "No, not really. Professor Novak slipped on a rock and hit his head. I *think* he hit his head. By the time two of his students had crawled into the chamber to get him out, he was delirious—wild-eyed and babbling something about seven tattooed men with obsidian knives. Constable Scobie fetched Doctor Fullsom, and Doctor Fullsom gave him something to calm him down. Dick felt better then, and he refused to let them take him to the hospital. He . . ." She turned, distracted by the ringing of the bell on the showroom door.

"Mr. Douglass?" It was a timid voice. "Are you there, Mr. Douglass?"

"Wirey?" Liss recognized the voice. It was Sonny's nurse. She waggled her eyebrows at Callie and moved to the showroom door. "What are you doing here?"

"Oh, thanks be! It's you I've been looking for, Melissa." Miss Wyre's thin face was pale above her narrow fur collar. Her hands fluttered. "Your mama thought you might be here. You must come home at once. I have the Chevy outside. Oh, do hurry! You may know places to look that we don't know about."

"Places to look for what?" asked Mr. Moon, gentling his voice to a small boom. "What's the problem?"

Miss Wyre put a gloved hand to her mouth. "Mr. Moon! I *am* sorry. I didn't see you. It's young Conway Tapp. He— oh, Melissa, dear! He's gone. Run away . . . or worse."

Liss squeezed her hand. "Oh, please don't flap now, Wirey. What's happened?"

"I don't know. It's all so confusing. Mrs. Calvert went out. She thought I was taking him his breakfast and lunch as usual, but I had left *very* early for East Liverpool to visit my sister. I *did* leave a note on the kitchen table to remind her, but Mrs. Calvert insists she never saw it. Oh dear, what *are* we to do?"

Mr. Douglass snorted and muttered, "They find that boy, he'll still be lost. A child can't grow without sunshine and a bit of room to stretch in, no more'n a plant." He raised his voice, shaking a finger at the rattled Miss Wyre. "Bend it too far from its own proper shape, it'll wither. Can't make a dahlia seed grow tea roses, can you? I remember his daddy. Same thing. This little one's his grand-daddy's sacrifice—to the times that're gone and his infernal pride."

"Whatever are you talking about?" Miss Wyre faltered. "Senator Tapp idolizes that child." She looked around wildly and was grateful when Liss called her back to the point.

"He's been gone since before breakfast? And nobody's missed him?" Liss was incredulous, but seeing Callie's ironic expression, supposed it was not so surprising after all—not with Grandfather out most of the day.

"He hadn't even gone to bed after his bath last night. He put a bolster under the covers to make it look as if he were sleeping, but the sheets were still fresh, you see. He hasn't been at all well." In her distress, Miss Wyre forgot her haste. "All those nightmares this past week! What should I have done? You don't suppose that . . ."

Liss and the other children were supposing, wildly. Liss remembered the dream about the seven 'doctors.' And what *had* Professor Novak seen? What if the Drip had been lured out again? The children whispered frantically among themselves. They would have to go back. The grownups, oblivious, soothed Miss Wyre.

"Miss Langley?" Callie pulled at her hand. "Miss Langley? When the professor thought he saw those tattooed men—when he was delirious, you know? Did he say anything about a kind of stone?"

"Why, yes." Miss Langley wondered at the urgency in her question. "One like the first he found. Two blue-green stones." She thrust a hand into her pocket. "I must return them. I had forgotten I had them."

Both stones lay in the palm of her hand: smooth, bright, no more than stones. She was holding them, and nothing had happened to her. It must be that the professor had felt their last flicker of power—Abáloc's reaching out.

"But then, we've no way back," Liss whispered.

17

Liss was miserable. She repeated to herself for the
twentieth time that it was all her fault. The snow
in the moonless wood was trampled almost smooth with all
the goings and comings. The sheriff's men and the state
police, and all the firemen for miles around, must have
tramped through the wood before they extended their
search eastward through the park and across the golf course
to the farmlands beyond. Liss directed the beam of her
flashlight up into the branches, but she was not really
searching. She had come just to come, to be away from
Grandfather pacing up and down by the telephone, demanding to know why the authorities weren't ringing up
every five minutes to keep him informed. Mama trotted
back and forth, alternatively soothing him and reassuring
Miss Wyre, who fell into hysterics every time the phone
did ring.

She stood beneath the old tree house and peered upward.
It had to be empty. They would have found him if he'd
been there. Someone had climbed up to look. She could
tell that whoever it was had been heavy, for all of the snow

had been knocked off the heavy lower branch. Idly, she ran her light along the wide cracks between the floorboards and saw something glitter in the passing beam. The spot of light wavered and returned to it. Cellophane? What from? It had not been there last time she was up.

Tucking the flashlight in her pocket, Liss scrambled up by feel alone, taking a nasty bump on her forehead in the process. The glitter turned out to be a tightly crumpled wad of kitchen foil that had been crammed down between the boards. Unwound, it spilled out breadcrumbs, twisted candy wrappers, and a tangle of rinds from sliced bologna onto the floor.

"He must've been here until everybody left the mound!" she said aloud. Puzzled, she turned the light up into the rafters and in a moment found another hoard jammed out of sight where two loose boards made a tiny "loft." It proved to be two pop bottles and a grubby notebook rolled up in a plaid car blanket. The last entry in the notebook read:

> *Thell come. They sayd they woud.
> I told them Pleas I want to be
> strongar then enyone. I hate everone
> becose they hate Me. Just wate. I
> will show them. Wen its dark They sed.
> P.S. I don't hate Ant Nan. I hate
> Missy mots of all.*

The flashlight dropped, rolling along the uneven floor and over the door's edge. Shoving the notebook and blanket into a corner, Liss backed out blindly and climbed down after it. She stumbled toward the mound.

"It's all my fault. I *knew* they were after him, but I didn't *think*." She came up against the chain-link fence and leaned there. "He was scared, and I only wanted to be shut of him. Mama's right." She sniffled, beginning to feel sorry for herself. "I was only thinking about me," she whispered, unaware that even now her concern was, deep down, more for herself than for Sonny. She banged her head against the fence, and it hurt so much that for a moment she could not catch her breath. Hanging there with her fingers laced in the heavy wire mesh, a little dizzy, she imagined that she heard a sound inside the enclosure—a cry from far off. Something there drew her, and she felt a pang, a pain below her heart as if something pulled at her there. But the fence was too high. And even if she could get in, there was no way back to Abáloc without the stones. They were useless—run down or turned off. Anyhow, they were just stones. "Just stones," she said aloud, not realizing.

"That you, Liss?" A voice was raised cautiously, and a small light switched on to shine in her eyes. It came from across the center of the mound, beyond the padlocked gate in the fence on the river side. "It's me, Callie." The shadow beckoned. "Meet you down at the graveyard end. It's important."

Liss's flashlight caught the figure hurrying along the fence opposite, and she moved to follow.

"Come on. Over the wall," Callie urged, scrambling up and dropping down on the far side. "They already looked for him here," she whispered. "It was on the six o'clock news. And nobody in Ridgeview can see our lights from here." She reached out a hand to Liss, who had gotten herself awkwardly hung up on the top of the wall. "We're s'posed to wait here."

Both switched their lights off.

"Wait? For what?"

"Well, Harry and me, we got to thinking, you know. What if it wasn't only just the stones? You recollect how Harry came that first time? It wasn't any stone."

Liss was silent for a moment. "But you and he are twins. It was probably that, don't you think?" She sounded almost hopeful.

"Maybe. I dunno. But, look: think about it *without* the stones. All three times. What else was there about all three times?"

The insistence, the excitement in her voice made Liss switch on the flashlight to see her face. "I give up. What?"

"Don't you see? Always somebody was reaching out, like, or just plain *needing*, and there wasn't anybody *there* to answer. Like Erilla and the book. Maybe the stone was only a kind of—sign. It was her reaching out, and we got tuned in kind of by accident. Don't you think? Like I was so scared and even if I didn't think about wishing for old Harry, there he was."

Liss did not answer for a long while. "You mean, if there's still a little corner of the Drip that's not such a rat, he might be reaching out that way? For me?" It was an uncomfortable thought. "I bet not. I bet he's either scared too spitless, or else he's *glad* he's got everybody in a flap. I tried to tune in on him once, really I did. The stinker got me all mushy, and then he laughed at me." She felt a guilty pang as the words came out. That had been the time he told her about the nightmare.

"You know," Callie said thoughtfully. "Sometimes I don't like you one little bit."

Fortunately, an owl hoot and an improbable whippoorwill broke the uncomfortable silence that followed. At the farthest downhill corner of the cemetery wall, lights appeared, and the scuffling sound of boots on stone was heard. Callie flashed her light once, and the others winked out. Whoever it was, they were feeling their way along the wall.

"We don't want the caretaker to see the lights," Harry whispered, coming up and crouching down beside Callie. Ralph, Pooch, and Sandy were close behind.

178

"Somebody turned up the hill just when I was on the wall," Sandy said. "Marie can't come. She has to baby-sit at home, and Erna doesn't have a telephone, so Mary Lou went down around her way."

"What's going *on?*"

"Liss?" A light winked briefly in Pooch's hand. "Why, it's a general meeting of the Two-O-Six REWTOF Club: Rescues Effected Without Thought of Fee."

Harry explained gruffly. "It's not just your bratty cousin. It's Abáloc. I got a feeling it's all connected somehow. Us and them. Maybe you and Callie did find this place by accident, but I don't think so. Doesn't it seem a little weird? I think it's almost like Apple Lock is repeating Abáloc, you know. Not exactly, but kind of. As if it's all slipped sideways. I mean, there's them with their books and all their past lost, and us with school all gummed up, and in a weird kind of way we rescue each other. I think it's the same with this. But it's sort of like—well, playin' basketball in the dark. You got to shoot as good as you can and just hope the basket's there." He leaned forward. "You go by feel and figuring. That's all you got."

"No. You got another choice," Callie amended. "No-show. Forfeit. What's it gonna be, Melissa?"

The waiting shadows had multiplied.

"Of course I'll go," Liss said in a small voice. "I was just too scared to go by myself. And I didn't understand. I couldn't go by myself. Don't you see?"

"Good enough." Harry punched her in the arm. "Let's go." He signaled downhill to the latest comers.

They slipped over the wall like one long, sinuous shadow. At the midpoint of the fence on the deep woods' side of the mound, they came to a halt while Harry and Ralph counted noses.

"Twenty-one. . . . Good, you got a shovel. Twenty-two. Hey, that can't be right." Ralph counted again.

"Erna couldn't come." It was Mary Lou's voice. "Her mama was working late, and she had to watch the kids."

"Then we ought to be twenty." Harry sounded suspicious, and everyone shifted uneasily. He switched his light on and swept it down the fence. A sharp-faced boy in an old cutdown hunting jacket jerked away, but then thought better of it and leaned back against the fence, grinning uncomfortably. The light glittered in his eyes.

Sandy made a face. "Wally Gowins!"

"The Dingaling Club, I presume?" Wally smirked.

"What are you doin' here, Gowins?" Pooch and Eddie closed in on him.

"He can't come," Liss wailed. "He'll ruin everything."

"Never trust a Gowins," Beverly Floyd said darkly. She wasn't quite sure why, but she had heard her father say it.

"Come on, you guys," Wally wheedled. "I just followed old Baker and Toohey. I thought they might be up to somethin', and I was right. If you're playin' at search party, I'm in. Or is it 'burgle some treasure'?" He leered unpleasantly. "You got to include me in, or I tell old goomer Scobie or that other cop you're up here."

"We could tie him to a tree," Jack Penrod suggested.

"I'd yell bloody murder." Wally smiled sweetly.

"We could always gag him," Ralph said. "But it isn't worth the ruckus he'd stir up after. Just everybody keep an eye on him. Who else we got here?" He flashed his light back the other way, past Mary Lou, who wore a blanket draped over her too-thin coat.

"Angela Paff!"

Everyone stared. There was Angela Paff. Blond ringlets, white bunny-fur hood, nose in the air, and all. At their stares, she blushed and began to look a little uncertain.

"Angela's family was at our house for dinner," Anne

Palisser said timidly. "When she asked to come to the 'meeting,' I couldn't think up a good excuse for not."

"And I'm staying. Please?" Angela Paff rarely said "please," except to teachers. She looked around at the hostile faces. "I've been awfully bored at St. Dunstan's," she offered. "Nothing ever happens there." It was the closest Angela could get to saying something nice.

Callie was the first to speak. "Well, I s'pose we could stand a little variety," she said solemnly.

Even Angela laughed.

They made it over the fence awkwardly but quickly, with Mary Lou's blanket doubled, then thrown over the top so that no one would get hung up on the stiff prickles of wire. Tank Sherman and Frank made themselves into a human stepladder, steadying and boosting the climbers. The boys went first and caught the girls as they wriggled over. Frank came last, tossing the shovel over before him.

"The altar stone! Is this it?" Teeny had climbed the mound and fallen into a shallow hole. Her voice quavered.

They turned their lights on it and saw one end of a large flat stone a little over four feet wide. A deep groove ran around the outer edge. It was only partially uncovered, for a large tree straddled the other end, gripping the stone with its roots.

"It must be."

"Give the shovel here," Harry commanded. "And one light's enough."

Wally Gowins bridled. "Who's *he* bossing around?"

"Me, for one, Melonhead. You got any objection?" Receiving no answer, Pooch bent to dig between the roots, loosening and scraping. "What are we looking for? Anybody know?" He shoveled loose dirt from the stone.

"Wait. Stop a minute!"

Liss scrambled down beside him and with her hands

scraped cautiously at the soft dark earth. A large clump fell away, and from beneath it she drew a dirty string. A few beads still dangled on it, and another glinted redly from a heap of dark dust on the stone. "It's my necklace," she whispered. "But how can it have gotten buried? It's my amber beads that belonged to Grandma Mitchell. He's smashed my beautiful beads! Why? Why would he smash them?"

Callie leaned down and shook her by the shoulder. "It's like the rabbit. Don't you see? The spite. That's how they got through. The snowmen . . . the kings. He couldn't *know* he was tuning them in."

"*This* isn't any bead." Pooch held up a blue-white aggie and then, scraping at the buried side of the stone, uncovered a cat's-eye and half of another marble. Liss reached out to brush away a small heap of earth and powdered glass and pull the empty wash-leather marble bag free. It was torn, mangled almost, as if it had been smashed at with a rock.

For a while no one noticed woods or sky. Uneasy, uncomfortable, unsure why they were there, they watched Liss's distress, and only gradually did they become aware of the soundless wind that blew outside their circle. The woods blew away, and the lights of the town below, and the winter's darkness shrank from the naked mound on the Field of Morning. Summer stars gleamed palely in a sky lightening faintly in the east. Sky and hill and the dark lands had a heaviness, a presence, a here-and-nowness that few of the children had ever felt so closely, so intensely; and yet it seemed at the same time distant, apart, unreachable—a land that did not know them, that did not show their footprints in the damp grass or in the dust of the new-built altarplace. Below, on the western side of the hill, the folk of Abáloc were gathered, a silent, somber crowd, listening to the man who spoke and watching the pale, shivering Moon Child who crouched on the stone. Amalahtis was there, and Erilla and Ayacas; but no Lincoas. Beyond the mound, on the far edge of the eastern hills, lights glittered—lamps and fires burning along the horizon, stretching away south.

"Throw off your grieving," Neolin called, reaching out his arms to the people. "We greet the Sun this day with a gift, for the Sun is made of fire and blood, and with such blossoms he must be fed! It is right! And if there *were* some slight wrong to regret in it, why, what of that? The watch-fires of the camp of the Seven Kings of Cibotlán fringe the sky. At sunrise the shadows of the Seven Kings shall reach even to the foot of this altar. But they wish to come to us as friends, not with a warring army. Their outriders await only this sign of our good will, of our affirmation of the Sun's power. Seeing that sign, they shall draw us within their circle of safety!"

Harry pushed forward in sharp protest. "Of submission, you mean! Safe like birds in cages! Safe like Tepollomis!"

The sky grew more pale, the air whiter. Neolin's voice railed on, and Harry knew no one had heard him. He cried out again, but his words fell into the white air as soundlessly as feathers.

"They can't see us," Callie said. "They can't see us. Turn on your lights. Everybody together. Oh, isn't there any way . . ."

But there was. Liss, moving jerkily, as if her will were still divided, reached her arms around the Moon Child, her cousin, to find that his stillness was the tautness of a spring too tightly wound. He whirled and clung to her so fiercely that it hurt.

Some in the crowd cried out, and Neolin turned to see what marvel they pointed to. Frightened, he stumbled backward. Someone nervously, without thinking, raised the chant, *"Tlegúro e záral ir miríguin num gualevóer!"* For to

183

them it seemed that two Moon Children knelt upon the Sun's altar, and around that altar hovered a great shadow —a crowd of half-seen, shifting shapes—and lights gleamed like bright holes in that darkness: moon and stars come down from the sky. As Callie and Harry knelt beside Liss, Neolin was gesturing wildly, groping in terror for some way to bend even this to his own purpose.

It was Harry who saw the distant movement, the flickering lights in the west. His heart flew to his throat. Time was too short for explanations. The sun beamed below the horizon. He leaped to his feet.

"Neolin is a fool who would be king," he cried, and the words came like silver, as if from some tongue other than his own. "The fool looks at the sun and is blinded, and he knows only its power and pain. But the sun is daybreak and morning, too, and green grass growing. See, there! Riding up the river out of the dark and into morning, day comes. Lincoas comes! He brings you other choices, morning choices. See there the daybreakers!"

As the folk turned spellbound away from Neolin toward the river, his, Harry's, voice became a whisper on the dawn wind, and the day broke upon them. On the pale ribbon of the beautiful river, a great flotilla of boats moved slowly upstream: strange boats, of a strange shape, and yet from them, faint at such a distance, a familiar song rose to the Field of Morning.

"Lincoas!" The cry was joy itself, and all the hillside joined the morning song.

18

Mr. Rivers yawned and turned off the eleven o'clock news. "A lot of excitement for one day, um? I guess all's well that ends well, as they say." He yawned again. "But I surely didn't think it was going to when I saw you chauffeured home in a police car. I thought it was trouble for certain! Come along, you two better get you off to bed, you hear? It's been a long, full day."

Callie and Harry protested. They were awake to the ends of their fingers, they said, and it would take even more than the "Late Show"—it was to be a Japanese monster movie—to put them to sleep.

Their mother uncurled from the sofa with a mock groan. "How can you bear those things? They're all alike."

"Yeah." Harry hunched over and walked with his knees bent. "The thing from the deep comes up outa the sea. It tromps down tall buildings with a single crunch! Bullets, gas, lasers, rockets—nothin' can dent it. The city's doomed!"

Callie scrunched down in her chair, laughing. "So they catch them a baby monster, and it roars its poor little roar and old Mama Monster goes sloshing back into the ocean, and the newspaper reporter marries the scientist's daughter. The End."

"All right. I can see you're surely a long way from sleep." Mrs. Rivers groped under the sofa for her shoes. "But get your pajamas on first, you hear? And be sure all the lights are off when you come up."

The eleven o'clock news had tried to make much of "the end of an adventurous day in Apple Lock," but it had to do so without the usual larding of eyewitness accounts. Old Senator Tapp had recorded his thanks to the searchers, but Constable Scobie and the Apple Lock Volunteer Fire Department had remained modestly silent. And not much wonder. In those unsettling moments on the Edge, they had exchanged nudges and meaning looks and without a word agreed to a man to keep some things back. How would it have sounded? They did not talk of it even among themselves, so that no one had to admit just how bewildered he was. Or, for that matter, that it had happened at all. For, while retracing their way along the Ridge, they had come to the deserted Edge to check the chambers in the mound one last time. Constable Scobie had a key to the padlocked gate, which he opened and carefully locked again after the men had made a thorough search. The padlock had snapped, and the searchers were headed for the road and cars and Thermoses of hot soup and coffee when the wind came up with a rush and clouds blew away from the moon, and they heard voices above them on the mound. Lights grew like flowers in the dark wood. Children. Dozens, it seemed. And the lost boy with them, wide-eyed and shivering under an old blanket. The constable had fumbled for his key and then fumbled with the lock. When the gate swung open, the children filed out, and the two search parties had eyed each other uncertainly. In the end, the children were ferried home, no questions asked.

"See, you can turn the sound off and just make up what they're saying." Harry sat up, turned the dial, and stretched out on the floor again.

"I bet that diver's going to . . . ha, yes! See, the rock'll start an avalanche and wake up the whatever-it-is."

Harry rolled over on his back, then arched up to pull his pajama top around straight. "I wish we knew what was gonna happen in Abáloc. Now we never will. I mean, all those boats, you know. Somehow I knew it was Lincoas, but who all was he bringing? He must've gotten help wherever he got all those boats. They were kind of weird boats—they looked *round*. Did you see? I wonder if there was a battle. They could've moved west, I suppose, or gone back to . . . what was it? The City of the Moon under the Mountain?"

Callie rested her chin on her hands and rubbed her toes in the shag rug. "Like Mr. Douglass says, nobody ever knows how anything's going to end, I s'pose. Not in Abáloc *or* Apple Lock." She watched the screen for a moment. "Now it's making waves. What do you bet it sinks the ship?"

Harry was thoughtful. "I guess if you knew *ahead* of time —even if it was going to be a good ending—it would kind of turn you off. Almost as much as if you thought everything always had to turn out lousy. You'd think it would happen even without your drop in the bucket." He sat up suddenly, startling Callie. "Man! You know, maybe there's really no such thing as endings. An ending's the beginning of something else, or maybe it's already the middle of something else. Or both."

"No pigeonholes!" Callie agreed, half mockingly. She switched off the television. "Still, we'll *be* here. We'll *see* what happens with Apple Lock—all that stuff Mr. Moon was talking about tonight—how maybe enough people are interested now not to grudge more money for the schools. And helping stop all the uglification. I'd like that. Maybe even a real museum we can help run. We're *here.* And there's no end of things to do. But . . ." Her fingers combed the rug. "I guess you get all twined up with people, even in a little while like we had in Abáloc, just by *doing* with them." She absentmindedly braided three strands of the rug together. "It would be nice to know . . . just a little. Just a hint."

Harry cleared his throat uncomfortably. It wasn't that he had not been thinking exactly the same thing, but what was the good of mooning about it? Girls never knew when to shut up. "What *I'd* like to know," he said nastily, "is how old Melissa Mitchell is gonna like living over in Poole with that wormy little kid, like her mother said they were going to, without any cooks and butlers and footmen—or whatever—to wipe his nose?"

Callie giggled in spite of herself. "She'll feel all noble and dedicated, maybe till Christmas. Then I guess she'll hate it and go around saying he's hopeless. But it'll be OK. After all, he can *only* get nicer."

Professor Novak switched off the eleven o'clock news and carried the cups to Miss Langley's kitchen, where she was rinsing out the cocoa pan.

"Guess I ought to be getting back, Josie," he said. "I have an eight o'clock class tomorrow, and another at eleven, so I won't be wangling lunch from you. Will you come up to the mound tomorrow afternoon, though?"

"Probably." Miss Langley dried her hands and followed him to the sitting room. "Don't forget your briefcase." She pointed. "It's down behind the chair. And here, you'd better take these before I forget them again." From her skirt pocket she drew the two blue-green stones.

"Thanks." He knelt to open the case. "When we have

everything catalogued, your Mr. Moon's people will have to decide what they want to sell and what to keep for his new museum, if he gets one."

"*Ours.* Everybody's," she corrected.

"Mm. Here, you might be interested in this." He undid the green cloth wrapping from a blackened wooden box and looked at her uncertainly, as if it were a peace offering and he wanted very much for her to be interested. "Do you know Professor Arthur at Poole? Classics Department? His son let me have this just for today, but I suppose he might be willing to loan it to an 'interested museum' sometime. I wanted to compare it with part of the design on that medallion your kids found. The workmanship is much finer than on the medallion. It's a strange story. Young Arthur claims it's from a cave somewhere in the Pennsylvania mountains. Place named Nūtāye? Something like that, anyway. It's a pretty thing, but we didn't have a clue what it was or whether it was genuine. The characters are untranslatable, and it might have been no more than an elaborate hoax. I'm afraid none of us took it very seriously until now. The question is, what was *this* doing under some Pennsylvania mountain?"

He handed it up to her.

The book inside the box had for covers polished plaques of rose crystal, and the clasp was like pale gold. The pages were covered with closely written signs in many colors. And on the first page was written:

"Why, it's beautiful!" Miss Langley ran a finger along the page's edge. "Will you leave it with me? Just until tomorrow?"

There was perplexity mixed with his pleasure. "Yes of course, but why?"

"Oh, no special reason. Only, I thought that Callie and Liss and Harry and the others might find it interesting."

They found it more than that. For an ending, it was full of middles and beginnings. . . .